"I wanted you as soon as I saw you glimmering across the room.

"I give you fair warning," he continued. "I'm hunting."

Her jaw dropped. Stunned, she stared at him, imprisoned by the implacable, leashed hunger of his eyes.

"At least you didn't say that you wouldn't sleep with me if I were the last man on earth."

"You're accustomed to that response?" she asked. "Then it's time you moved up to a better class of mistress. Not me—I'm sorry, I'm too busy at the moment."

"So much for honesty," Clay said ironically, and once more tightened his arms around her.

To her intense humiliation Natalia's body betrayed her. Although superhuman will held back her rash impulse to signal surrender, she had to fight a bitter battle with untamed need—and he, damn him, knew it!

ROBYN DONALD has always lived in Northland in New Zealand, initially on her father's stud dairy farm at Warkworth, then in the Bay of Islands, an area of great natural beauty, where she lives today with her husband and an ebullient and mostly Labrador dog. She resigned her teaching position when she found she enjoyed writing romances more, and now spends any time not writing in reading, gardening, traveling and writing letters to keep up with her two adult children and her friends.

Books by Robyn Donald

Don't miss any of our special offers. Write to us at the following address for information on our newest releases.

Harlequin Reader Service
U.S.: 3010 Walden Ave., P.O. Box 1325, Buffalo, NY 14269
Canadian: P.O. Box 609, Fort Erie, Ont. L2A 5X3

Robyn Donald

A RELUCTANT MISTRESS

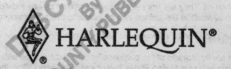

HARLEQUIN®

TORONTO • NEW YORK • LONDON
AMSTERDAM • PARIS • SYDNEY • HAMBURG
STOCKHOLM • ATHENS • TOKYO • MILAN • MADRID
PRAGUE • WARSAW • BUDAPEST • AUCKLAND

For Barbara and Peter Clendon. The best of friends
and booksellers extraordinaire. Thank you.

3 3113 02032 4051

ISBN 0-373-12162-8

A RELUCTANT MISTRESS

First North American Publication 2001.

Copyright © 1999 by Robyn Donald.

Visit us at www.eHarlequin.com

Printed in U.S.A.

PROLOGUE

STANDING in a land agent's office pretending to check out a couple of likely prospects, Clay Beauchamp looked up sharply when a low, husky laugh teased his ears.

Outside in the street a woman had stopped to talk, and the smoky sensuality of her voice homed straight through his defences, waking his male response to instant, lustful life.

The subtropical sun of an early Northland autumn picked out a head of curls black as a sinful midnight; they looked as though she'd taken to them in exasperation with a blunt pair of scissors, but the bad cut only emphasised their springy vitality. As Clay's eyes narrowed, she turned her head.

His stimulated hormones surged into clamorous over-drive. Deliberately controlling his physical arousal, he surveyed a face made to star in erotic dreams.

Not that she was pretty—or even beautiful. No, she possessed something much rarer than either—a cool, guarded sensuality produced by the happy genetic accident of a softly voluptuous mouth and large eyes set on a provocative slant. The tempting, tantalising combination of mouth and eyes overshadowed ivory skin and neat, regular features.

Moving slightly so that his unbidden and uncomfortable response was partly hidden by the sheaf of papers in his hand, Clay studied her with speculative, intent interest. Five feet eight, he estimated, with wide shoulders and curved hips that hinted at a generous sexuality—and although she spoke with a New Zealand accent he'd bet some intriguing bloodlines mingled in that lithe, long-legged body.

The man she was talking to interrupted, laughing. Clay

frowned. Without the play of speech her face settled into a watchful, disciplined wariness that denied access to her thoughts and emotions.

But that mouth! Full and red and eager when she relaxed, it summoned all too vivid images. What would it take to see that restraint shattered in passion? Sweat beaded Clay's temples and his breath strangled in his throat as his body reacted with violent enthusiasm to the thought.

Helen of Troy, he thought with annoyed irony, had probably had the same effect on the men who had desired her.

'She's a looker, isn't she?'

The land agent's nasal voice broke Clay's concentration. Irritated that he'd been caught staring at an unknown woman with the fervour of a stag in rut, he asked curtly, 'Who is she?'

'Natalia Gerner. Her father bought a chunk of Pukekahu Station—it's the second in the file. Yeah, that one—' he said as Clay shuffled the papers.

The land agent went on, 'Would have been about thirteen years ago, when old Bart Freeman from Pukekahu had the Inland Revenue Department hot on his trail for unpaid taxes and he had to find money damned fast. The only way he could come up with the cash was to cut off several parcels of land. Natalia's father—straight from Auckland, never been on a farm in his life before!—bought one, gave it some damned stupid poetic name and did his best to railroad himself into bankruptcy.'

He snorted as Natalia Gerner laughed outside the small office, the liquid feminine sound sheer enticement. Clay continued looking at the paper in his hand, but the words blurred as every sense sharpened. Resolutely he overrode the unruly demands of his body, forcing his mind back to the business at hand. He'd come here for a specific purpose, and nothing was going to get in his way.

The land agent continued, 'Mind you, they had bad luck too—her mother died when Natalia was eighteen, then her father dropped dead of a heart attack—three years ago it'll be now. If you decide on Pukekahu—and you'll never get land in the North cheaper—she'll be your neighbour.'

Clay frowned, striving to push Natalia Gerner's exotic face and sexy laugh to the back of his mind. This was business, and no woman—not even one with a face like a courtesan and a body that hinted at all sorts of decadent pleasures—interfered with his business.

Actually, this was more than business. It was the culmination of years of quiet, persistent, ruthless effort and struggle. He tamped down the flicker of triumph even as he felt it. However leggy and tormenting, the woman with a laugh like Eve wasn't going to cloud his brain today.

The land agent grinned, his middle-aged face sly. 'She's a very generous girl, they say. She and Dean Jamieson—that's the vendor—had a good thing going there a while back, but it fizzled out.'

Life had taught Clay that too much emotion led to grief and defeat; over the years he'd learned how to discipline his responses, even his pleasures. Yet he had to pretend to read the page of figures and stare at the photograph of a huge Victorian villa in the last stages of disintegration while he struggled to restrain a red tide of rage.

The land agent gave a snort of laughter. 'She probably thought she had it made then, but he wasn't going to break up his marriage for her. I heard she got greedy and wanted him to pay her debts off. I don't blame her—why shouldn't she get the best out of the situation?'

Clay's memory summoned only too vividly a seductive mouth, green eyes and skin like ivory silk, a lithe body. His treacherous mind also summoned other images—ones he banished, but not before heat clamped his body, subduing the processes of his brain with a surge of raw lust.

When he could trust his voice he asked abruptly, 'Why is Jamieson selling Pukekahu?'

He'd already flown over the cattle station, so he knew these photographs had been taken in a very good light—

possibly even doctored a little. The paddocks he'd seen hadn't had fertiliser on them for far too many years.

The older man shrugged. 'He's one of the South Island Jamiesons,' he said. 'His stepmother—she was Bart Freeman's daughter—left him Pukekahu when she died, but I suppose it's too far from his other holdings to make it worth his while to keep it.'

It had, however, Clay thought savagely, been worth his while to strip the place of everything of value, running it down so that it was now worth practically nothing. Yes, Dean would have enjoyed that; it would have satisfied his mean, petty soul.

Perhaps misunderstanding Clay's continued silence, the land agent said quickly, 'He's a very willing vendor.'

Another throb of feminine laughter turned both male heads. Coldly angry with himself, Clay wrenched his attention back to the papers in his hand.

Grinning, the older man revealed, 'That's Pukekahu's farm manager she's talking to. I doubt if he'll stay the course. Not enough money, for a start—Phil's never going to be more than a manager. He's good, mind you. If you buy the station you couldn't do better than keep him on, but he has to be told what to do. Easy meat for Natalia; she'll be bored soon. Won't take her long to find someone new— there's always been men buzzing around her.'

Disgusted because he wanted to hear about the woman who was still smiling at Phil Whoever-he-was—even more disgusted because he wanted to claim that smile, that fascinating, vital face, that strong, delectable body—and thoroughly furious at the flare of raw jealousy that sliced through him, Clay said evenly, 'If I buy Pukekahu it will be because it fits into my portfolio, not because the woman next door is promiscuous.'

The land agent's face flushed in unpleasant patches. 'Of course,' he blustered. 'Anyway, I didn't say she was promiscuous! She's had a rough spin, that girl...'

Something in Clay's face must have alerted him because

he stumbled on, 'Her father left her with a tunnel-house set-up and debts so big she'll probably still owe money when she's fifty. The only thing she's got in her favour is her looks, and I don't blame her for setting her sights high enough to get herself out of hock. Still, if anyone can make it she will; she's always been tough and stubborn and she's a damned hard little worker.'

So she had more than her looks in her favour. Pity about the mercenary streak...

Clay set a discarded sheet of paper down on the desk and pretended to study the next. In a barely interested voice he asked, 'Why's she paying off her father's debts? She isn't legally obliged to unless they were partners.'

The agent shook his head. 'Her father borrowed from his friends to set up the tunnel-houses. He planned to grow orchids, but—story of his life!—he was too late for the boom years. When he died Natalia sold just about everything that wasn't nailed down and realized enough to pay off some of the debt, but the major creditors are an elderly couple. If she reneged on the rest of the loan they'd be left with practically nothing.'

So the carmine-lipped houri had a conscience—an over-active one if it had led to her mortgaging her future for the sake of an elderly couple. Suppressing an odd protective-ness, Clay said curtly, 'All right, tell me why I should buy Pukekahu.'

This was what he'd come for, this derelict cattle station. That was why he'd chosen this small-town agent who'd probably never heard of his company, Beauchamp Holdings, because nothing would give Dean Jamieson more pleasure than to ratchet up the price of Pukekahu if he knew Clay was buying it.

In fact, he'd probably refuse to sell the place to him, even though he needed the money desperately.

Clay wanted Pukekahu with a hunger that was based on

that most dangerous of emotions, revenge, but he didn't plan to pay a cent more than it was worth.

And he had no intention of letting the fact that Natalia Gerner lived half a mile from its front gate affect him.

CHAPTER ONE

'LIZ, I can't go.' Natalia Gerner rubbed at her brows, erasing a frown. The other hand clenched more tightly around the telephone.

'Why not?' her best friend demanded.

'I haven't got a partner, for a start.' Let alone a dress suitable to wear to a masquerade—a masquerade *ball*, for heaven's sake! What had possessed the Rotary and Lions Clubs to sponsor a masquerade ball? Reining in her frustration, Natalia tried to sound reasonable and practical. 'This is New Zealand, not Regency England, and here in Bowden we entertain with barbecues. If we can cook we do dinner parties. Whatever, we don't do balls.'

Her friend laughed. 'Don't be so curmudgeonly—it doesn't sit well on twenty-three-year-old shoulders. It'll be a real hoot. Mum and Dad have organised a party, and you have to come. You won't need a partner; Greg's home, and he adores dancing with you. Mind you, so does everyone else—you dance like a dream.'

'I used to do a mean tango,' Natalia admitted. Her heavy-lidded gaze lifted to the window, dwelt a moment on the curved, half-moon tunnels covered in white plastic, and packed full of capsicum plants, then moved on to the paddock where a very small herd of beef cattle grazed placidly in the winter sun.

Liz had never been one to give up easily. 'We're not going to do minuets and country dances, for heaven's sake. And you—of all people—can't have forgotten how to fox-trot and stuff.'

'I probably have.'

Trenchantly, Liz retorted, 'It's like swimming and riding

11

a bike—you never forget—so stop wimping out. Your father would hate to hear you say no to an evening of fun. And so would your mother.'

Natalia closed her eyes. One of the disadvantages of their long friendship was Liz's unerring aim at her weakest spots.

With ruthless accuracy Liz went on, 'And don't tell me you haven't got a dress to wear. Remember the silk one I bought in Auckland last year because I hoped it would make my eyes the same colour as yours? Well, you can wear that.'

'You have beautiful eyes,' Natalia said feebly, knowing she was losing the battle.

'Possibly, but we both know they're not in the same league as yours! I was going to give you that dress before I went to England, anyway.' Her voice altered. 'Nat, do come. We'll have a great time. The Barkers have opened their ballroom and—'

'I can't afford it,' Natalia interrupted.

After a short silence, Liz said, 'We'll pay. Nat, please don't let pride stand in your way—you know you'd do the same for me.'

Natalia chewed her lip. 'That's not fair.'

'Vowing to be eternal best friends on our first day of school gives me the right to be unfair. Ever since your father died you've buried yourself up on your hill like Rumpelstiltskin.'

'You've got the wrong fairy tale. I don't ask riddles and threaten to kidnap babies. And I certainly don't spin straw into gold.' Which would have been immensely useful these past three years.

Liz, being Liz, didn't accept her unspoken capitulation, but insisted on dotting 'i's. 'You held my hand through a couple of broken hearts and assorted childhood traumas—won't you at least let me do this?'

'That's two hundred per cent not fair!'

'But you're going to give in to emotional blackmail, aren't you?'

Natalia unclenched her fingers from the telephone. 'How much are the tickets?'

'I'm not going to tell you.' Real exasperation snapped through Liz's tone. 'If you're determined to be sticky about it, consider yours a birthday present.' She laughed. 'Come on, Nat—stay the night, and we'll get ready together and giggle and pretend we're seventeen instead of twenty-three, and that I'm not heading off to Oxford to bury myself in mediaeval English texts, and you're not stuck in Bowden working your heart out because of some quixotic belief that you're responsible for your father's debts. For one night we'll pretend that our lives are going to be the way we wanted them to be when we planned them at high school. Do you remember—I was going to marry Jason Wilson and have his children? And you were going to be a botanist and paint exquisite pictures of native plants. That, of course, was *before* you fell in love with Simon Forsythe in the seventh form!'

Natalia had to force a laugh. 'All right, all right, I'll come,' she said, 'but only because I want to see Mr Stephens from the garage in a mask. And I'll get dressed at your place. I won't be able to stay, though, because I've got to catch the early transport to the markets.'

'I knew you'd do it,' Liz said warmly. 'You need some fun, and we'll have it, I promise. And don't worry about a mask, either—I've got the perfect one for you!'

Sequinned and frivolous, the exact green of her eyes, the perfect mask flaunted exotic feathers that winged out against Natalia's black curls. It matched Liz's discarded silk dress, the most glamorous thing Natalia had ever worn. Demure of neckline in the front, the back swooped down past her shoulder blades towards a nipped-in waist, below which the skirts frou-froued, stopping short enough to reveal a lot of Natalia's legs.

'Stop jittering!' Liz commanded. 'No, you can't wear a bra with it, but you look great without one, and, yes, it's short, but you've got truly excellent legs. It's very, very sexy—I knew it would suit you.' Without chagrin, Liz smoothed her own slinky black dress before adjusting her black and white mask. 'But then, everything does. It's those fine, aristocratic features. They fool everyone into thinking you're a sweetly pretty girl—until they get a load of those wicked, come-hither eyes.'

'Come-hither! In other words, I've got heavy eyelids. You've been reading Regency books again,' Natalia accused, laughing. 'I'll bet your supervisor didn't know you devoured popular fiction when she steered you into first-class honours with your MA.'

'I *like* Regencies,' Liz told her unrepentantly. 'I have this thing for tall, dark, handsome, very rich aristocrats.'

'You might find one in England.'

Liz sighed. 'I don't think they breed them any more.'

As they walked into the splendid ballroom in the district's biggest homestead, Natalia said, 'How mysterious and interesting we look. Perhaps we should go around in masks all the time!'

The rest of their party trooped in after them in a cloud of laughter and conversation. 'Hmm, yes, very mysterious—and ultra-sexy. Even Greg,' Liz added, casting a quick glance at her brother.

'He's a very handsome man,' Natalia said lightly.

'But not for you.' Liz had made no attempt to hide her wish that her favourite brother and her best friend might one day fall in love.

'No.'

'Ah, well, perhaps you'll meet some gorgeous hunk tonight.' Liz gazed openly around, waving to friends, smiling. 'I can't see one,' she murmured, 'but there's Mr Stephens with the Barkers, Nat—and he looks pretty good in a mask!'

Halfway through the evening Natalia admitted that Liz had been right to nag her to come. She'd had a great time, dancing with old friends and flirting lightly with several newcomers, talking to people she hadn't seen for months.

Waiting until her latest partner had set off to rejoin his wife, Liz hissed, 'He's here!'

'Who?' Natalia lifted her glass of iced water.

'The hunk we ordered. Sidle a look towards the door. You can't miss him.'

More to humour her than anything, Natalia set her glass down and turned her head.

The stranger was definitely unmissable, partly because he was a head above most of the other men. At least six foot three, Natalia estimated, with shoulders in proportion and an air of cool command that dominated the room.

Severe black and white evening clothes contrasted magnificently with golden skin. Light gleamed on wavy black hair, highlighted an autocratic, hawk-nosed face with a square, slightly cleft chin and a wide mouth. Long-legged, narrow-hipped, a conventional black mask emphasising those strong features, the stranger could have walked out of one of Liz's Regency novels—or an X-rated myth.

He was talking to a woman Natalia didn't know, a well-rounded creature whose scarlet mask—scattered with tiny chips of mirror glass—couldn't conceal her look of desperate anticipation, as though she'd just found water in the Sahara.

Natalia didn't blame her. The stranger's height and archetypal, dangerous good looks made him stand out, but what compelled attention was his air of vibrant, vital sexuality, a coiled, dynamically masculine magnetism. He had the invisible aura of a man who knew he was attractive to the opposite sex—an inbuilt confidence that set her teeth on edge.

Fanning herself with vigour, Liz made a noise like a vocal leer. 'I need a cold shower,' she growled. 'Do you know him?'

'Never seen him before.'

Liz grinned. 'He's looking at you.'

'Hope he likes my profile, then,' Natalia said, turning to smile ironically at her friend. 'Yes, he's gorgeous, but men like that have wives, or very glamorous girlfriends who work in television. Guaranteed. Perhaps the woman with him?'

'A cynical little statement, but you could be right, alas.' Liz sighed. 'However, if he asks me to dance I'm not going to let any possible girlfriend concern me. I don't think he looks married.'

'Neither did the last hunk I met at a party,' Natalia said softly, icily.

Liz sighed. 'Sorry, love, I'd forgotten about Dean Jamieson. Which is what you should do.'

'I try, but it's not often a man thinks that the excitement and privilege of sleeping with him should outweigh a few inconveniences like a wife.' Natalia reined in the anger that still fired her temper whenever she thought of the man who owned the property next door. 'The only thing that comforts me about that situation is the look on his face when I said, no, thank you, I have this strange, old-fashioned idea that marriage means trust and fidelity, so although you're a very sexy man I'm not going to bed with you!'

'He was a rat,' Liz soothed. 'You know, I suppose it never occurred to Dean that you'd find out he was married. Just as well my mother has this network of old friends the full length of New Zealand, or you might have been really hurt.'

Natalia shrugged. 'He hurt my pride and dented my heart a little, that's all.'

'More than a little, I think.'

Natalia looked down at her restless fingers in her lap. 'I was an idiot,' she said quietly. 'I suppose I thought he was Prince Charming, and that he might be the one to whisk me off and marry me and rescue me from my life of drudgery. He was funny and intelligent and very attractive, and he seemed genuine.'

'I'm sure he was genuine.' Liz's tone was both under-standing and crisp. 'He saw a woman he wanted, and he didn't care whether he broke your heart provided he got you.'

'He didn't break my heart,' Natalia said steadily.

'I know,' Liz said. 'You've got too much sense to let an attack of wishful thinking blind you for too long.'

'Thanks for the vote of confidence.' But Liz didn't know just how close she'd come to succumbing to Dean Jamieson's practised charm.

'Think nothing of it.'

Natalia said evenly, 'What really makes me mad is that he told everyone in Bowden that I knew he was married.'

'It was a lousy, malicious, petty thing to do, but at least you know what sort of man he is.'

'You're so right. A snake. One I came perilously close to falling for, which gives me a very low opinion of my intelligence!'

Liz primmed her mouth and endeavoured to look affected—difficult when her small face was alight with laughter. 'Anyone can be taken in once. The important thing is to not let it happen again.' She relaxed into a sly grin. 'So I'll do my best to find out who the newcomer is, and whether he's got an encumbrance. I don't think the woman with him is his—she's too hungry. And he doesn't look like a man who believes in abstinence.'

Half an hour later, as Natalia was coming back into the ballroom after a swift visit to the cloakroom, she was hailed by an old friend, a man who'd been a couple of classes ahead of her at school. They were laughing together when his wife of six months arrived with the speed, determination and subtlety of a mother rhinoceros seeing a lion examine her infant.

Cold-eyed, proprietorial, she snapped out a thin smile. 'Hello, Natalia, nice to see you. Max, why don't we dance this one?'

He looked embarrassed, and suddenly shifty. 'Oh, yes, of course,' he said. 'See you around, Nat.'

Natalia's lashes drooped as his wife all but dragged him

away. Damn Dean Jamieson and his lies. How long was it
going to take her to live down the reputation he'd deliberately saddled her with?

'He *might* see you around,' a disturbing masculine voice
murmured from behind her, 'but not if she sees you first.'

Stiff with pride, Natalia turned abruptly, only to collide
with a large, immovable object. Before she had a chance to
trip, hands clamped just above her elbows. Powerful fingers
held her for a moment, startlingly tanned against her pale
skin.

Of course she knew who it was.

'Sorry,' she muttered, lifting her head to look the stranger
in the eyes.

Their impact drove the breath from her lungs. Behind the
black silk mask, narrowed tawny-gold slivers were fringed
by black lashes in a watchful, almost calculating scrutiny.
In spite of that, Natalia was left in no doubt that he liked
what he saw.

On the right-hand side of his face a thin, faded scar
slashed downwards to the point of his jaw. Although it
heightened the forceful, uncompromising power of his
honed features, Natalia had to stop herself from tracing it
with a finger.

Latent sensation flamed into life inside her—a volatile
mixture of fire and ice, honey and gall, velvet and steel that
combined in a fierce, terrifyingly elemental hunger.

'I'm sorry—I knocked you,' the unsmiling stranger said.

'No, it was my fault—I wasn't looking where I was going,' she returned, reckless in her desire to get away.

One hand slid down her forearm. As she stared, dumb-
struck, lean fingers rested on her pulse, testing the rapid,
heavy throbbing of her heartbeat in the fragile blue veins.

Face hot, she wrenched free; he didn't try to hold her.

'You can feel mine if you like. It's beating just as fast as
yours,' he purred, his devil-dark voice pierced by a shock-
ingly intimate note.

She couldn't breathe. Perhaps this was an asthma attack;

she'd heard they could come on like this, unexpected, terrifying...

'No, thanks,' she said, appalled by her unsure tone.

His laughter shivered through her, stroked her slowly, as sensuous as sleek fur against her skin.

'Dance with me,' he said, and without waiting for her answer took her hand in his and led her to the floor.

Later she wondered what on earth he'd done to her, why she hadn't walked away from him back to her own party. Perhaps the old-fashioned waltz had cast some old-fashioned spell on her, melting her into docility.

Turning her into his arms with practised skill, he swept her on to the floor. Of course he was a brilliant dancer.

As ravishing Viennese music filled the room, Natalia's brain switched off. For the first time in her life she experienced the mindless pull of desire, existing only through her senses—senses swamped by the man who guided her through the crowds on the floor. Lost in a silent, erotic fantasy, they danced the whole set without speaking.

Until the music changed she'd begun to think he was never going to speak; then, as though that wordless, fiercely intent communion had never happened, he said, 'I'm Clay Beauchamp, and you're Natalia Gerner.'

Like its owner, his voice had immediate impact. Its masculine depth—emphasised by an undertone of raw strength—lifted the hair on the back of Natalia's neck as she retorted, 'And I don't like being ordered to dance.'

Although she was staring rigidly over his shoulder she caught a flash of white teeth when he smiled. 'I'll remember that in future.' The fingers around hers tightened fractionally, then loosened.

Natalia stiffened and almost missed a step. 'Sorry,' she said tonelessly.

'My fault,' he said, and pivoted with a lithe masculine grace.

As they spun she realised he'd used the steps to pull her a little closer. Clay Beauchamp was too sophisticated for the usual overt manoeuvres of men looking for a cheap thrill and a taste of sexual power. His grip was relaxed enough to allow her the illusion of freedom, yet for a suffocating second she felt as though he'd caged her.

It gave her such a shock she lifted her head and pulled back.

When he smiled one corner of his mouth lifted a little higher than the other, giving him a slightly lopsided look that should have reduced that potent male attraction. At the very least he should have looked endearing.

Except that 'endearing,' she thought, watching the hard curve of that classically carved mouth, was not a word she'd ever associate with this man.

For the first time in her life, Natalia tripped on the dance floor.

'Sorry,' Clay Beauchamp murmured, gleaming topaz eyes raking her face as he supported her. 'And we were doing so well, I'd even stopped counting one-two-three.'

He waltzed as though he'd been born in Vienna. And he was really getting to her. Time for damage control.

With the cool politeness her mother had drummed into her, she asked, 'Are you a visitor here, Mr Beauchamp?'

'Temporarily.' Amusement deepened his voice.

Natalia hoped she wasn't spoiled or over-confident, but she'd never been laughed at before. It was a challenge she should refuse.

Unfortunately she'd always found it almost impossible to back away from a dare. Lifting her lashes, she surveyed the powerful, angular face with a glinting appreciation. 'But surely all visitors are temporary?' she asked demurely, knowing the moment she'd spoken that she'd made an error of judgement.

This man wasn't the sort you teased.

'Not in this case. I've bought Pukekahu Station,' he said indolently.

Guilt roiled with anger and settled icily in her stomach. Resisting it—for what had she to feel guilty about?—Natalia directed a slanting glance at the angular face above hers. 'How appropriate. You've got the right eyes for a place that's called the Hill of Hawks.' She was dicing with danger, yet she couldn't have banished the mockery that flicked through her words.

Outlined with sinister exactness by the black mask, those golden eyes narrowed. 'And the right nose too.'

Common sense kicking in too late, Natalia forced her voice into an approximation of friendly interest. 'It's going to take you a while to bring Pukekahu into profit again. Even the house is falling down. Are you planning to live there?'

'I live in Auckland.'

She didn't like the silences: they sizzled with tension. 'Unusual place for a farmer to live,' she said lightly.

'I'm not exactly a farmer. More an agri-businessman.'

'Ah, one of the new breed of absentee landlords,' she returned affably. 'As I said, temporary.'

Her hand—loose on his shoulder—registered a sudden tightening of muscles beneath the superb cloth of his dinner jacket. It lasted for a second only, but she was recklessly pleased that she'd got through his formidable armour.

'I've never heard myself described as an absentee landlord before,' he drawled. 'I prefer to think I'm part venture capitalist, part restorer of over-stocked farmland.'

'How altruistic.' Her tone oozed blandness, but he'd have had to be stupid not to recognise the caustic lash to each word. And Natalia would bet her next year's income that Clay Beauchamp wasn't stupid.

'You're an entrepreneur yourself, I believe,' he said obliquely. 'Bowden's capsicum queen, who just happens to share a boundary with Pukekahu.'

It took all her will to say in a bright voice, 'I'm flattered, but "capsicum queen" doesn't quite cut it. There's something inherently unromantic about peppers, don't you think? Perhaps it's their shape—so sturdy and blocky.'

'Are you a romantic, Natalia?' Clay Beauchamp asked with a subtle, predatory inflection.

Her fault; she'd given him the perfect opening. 'Not in the least,' she returned crisply, smiling with sunny nonchalance into his face.

For several seconds he and Natalia duelled, using those most potent of weapons, the eyes. Natalia refused to lower her lashes; in the end he won by the simple trick of dropping that tawny gaze to her mouth.

Not fair, she thought, irrationally elated—but not surprising either. Clay Beauchamp probably never played fair.

'Good,' he said enigmatically. 'Romantics are a real nuisance. And, speaking as an unromantic male, do you wear contact lenses to brighten the colour of those magnificent eyes?'

Until then she hadn't realised that she was rather proud of her eyes, but what really flicked that pride was that he'd noticed.

Well, she could salvage something. With a deliberate sweep of her lashes, she allowed her gaze to rest a significant moment on the hard line of his jaw and purred, 'You can't really expect me to admit to that. However, I'll confess that I wear lipstick.'

'So you're a tease,' he said, his smile a swift, savage punishment. 'I'm disappointed—you seem more direct, more open.'

Anger glittered in the depths of her eyes, licked in a flame across her cheekbones. With that cat-like smile still pinned to her lips, she said, 'I'm every bit as frank as you are.' There, that should shut him up, because if ever a man held secrets close to his chest this one did.

'I doubt it.' Beneath the silk mask his intent stare was pure gold. Without breaking eye contact he pivoted gracefully, and this time the hand across her back came to rest on the heated skin just above her waist.

Although Clay released her almost immediately, and his hand left her skin for a more discreet position, its imprint burned like a brand. Tension sawed through her nerves, producing a feverish need.

Calmly he said, 'I want you, Natalia. I wanted you as soon as I saw you glimmering like a serpent woman across the room. I give you fair warning—I'm hunting.'

Her jaw dropped. Stunned, she stared at him, imprisoned by the implacable, leashed hunger of his eyes.

'Not so open, after all,' he murmured, a taunting amusement not warming his expression. 'At least you didn't say that you wouldn't sleep with me if I were the last man on earth.'

Her brain began to work again, overriding the violent pulse of desire. 'You're accustomed to that response?' she asked, arching her brows in pretended surprise. 'Then it's time you moved up to a better class of mistress. Not me— I'm sorry, I'm too busy at the moment—but I can introduce you to several women who might be interested.' In spite of her attempt at sophisticated repartee she couldn't banish the bite from her words.

What was it about her that made men think she was easy? Dean had expected her to fall into bed with him, been angry when she refused.

Clay's long black lashes half covered his eyes. He laughed, a sound that battered the remnants of her composure. 'So much for honesty,' he said ironically, and once more tightened his arms so that for a second she was held inexorably against him. Still dancing with a lithe masculine grace, still in perfect time to the music, he forced her to accept the reality of his lean, aroused body.

To her intense humiliation, Natalia's betrayed her. In her hidden, inner reaches desire worked its physical magic, overwhelming her in a smooth, heated tide. Although superhuman will held back her rash impulse to signal a surrender, she had to fight a bitter battle with untamed need— and he, damn him, knew it!

She'd been attracted to Dean—but this was a wilder, fiercer response, and it scared her. This, she thought, trying desperately to regroup her defences, was the sort of thing that toppled kingdoms.

Clay relaxed his grip. 'Physical evidence is more trust-worthy than words. They often deceive—the body never does.'

If there had been the slightest satisfaction—the faintest note of smugness—in his voice, Natalia would have twisted free and stalked across the crowded dance floor to the other side of the room. What stopped her was the raw catch to his words, the harsh, startled edge he couldn't conceal. When she looked up, darkness prowled the golden eyes.

And that made her angrily, foolishly confident. Carefully she uncurled the fingers that had dug into his upper arm. Carefully she positioned her gaze over his shoulder.

People moved in a bright kaleidoscope of colour around the floor, the masks turning familiar faces to strangers. Chat-ter and laughter echoed in her ears, backed by the succulent, achingly poignant sound of a turn-of-the-century waltz—one of her mother's favourites.

Coolly, deliberately, she asked, 'Is this your usual mode of attack? A pre-emptive strike with no attempt at subtlety? What follows now—all-out war?'

His tight smile revealed strong white teeth that snapped out one word. 'Surrender.'

CHAPTER TWO

NATALIA should have laughed in his face. She should have said, Really? with every ounce of sarcasm she could muster, lifted her brows in scorn and disdain and left Clay there in the middle of the dance floor.

Instead her mouth dried and she felt as though she'd fallen into a black hole and was being torn apart by forces she couldn't fight. Beneath that succinct word there had been a controlled, menacing determination, the remorseless patience of the hunter he'd likened himself to.

She was frightened. She was exhilarated. And that reckless excitement wasn't tempered by common sense or pragmatism. He'd issued a challenge, one she was so tempted to take up she could taste the wanting—keen, enticing, insistent, dangerous as a drug.

'I'm not into surrender,' she parried, surprised to hear a steady voice.

Clay swung her around a couple who'd forgotten their neighbours were watching and were swaying together in an embrace that came close to being embarrassing. 'Perhaps I am,' he said, and laughed quietly at the swift flash of fire in her glance. 'Yes, you'd like that, wouldn't you, Natalia,' he said, reading her so perfectly that it was a statement, not a question.

'I'm *very* into power,' she said offhandedly.

But that terrifying, untamed desire stirred again. She felt as though he'd put his mark on her; his scent, fiercely male, filled her nostrils; her fingers tingled, seeking slick, tanned skin. And sensation flowed through her, glowing, fiery, merciless as lava, devouring everything in its path.

This is simple lust, Natalia thought disdainfully, nothing

25

more. Intensely relieved when at last the music died on a flourish, she pulled free of his arms, turning her head away in the hope of disguising the hasty flutter of her breathing.

'It cuts both ways,' Clay Beauchamp said unhurriedly, tawny eyes glittering as he held out his arm.

If only her mother hadn't been so determined to bring up her daughter as a lady! Reluctantly Natalia put the tips of her fingers on his sleeve, straightening her spine as they walked across to the side of the room.

Liz was already sitting there; horrified, Natalia endured a sharp stab of jealousy at her friend's sunny, unaffected smile at Clay.

Woodenly, she introduced them. 'Liz, this is Clay Beauchamp, who has bought Pukekahu Station. Clay, Liz Kaiwhare. Her parents own the Tourist Lodge in Manakiwi Bay.'

Dimpling, Liz held out her small hand. With a smile that indicated more than appreciation, Clay took it. Another spear of jealousy rankled through Natalia.

'You looked wonderful together,' Liz said with a rare lack of tact. 'Everyone was watching you—you're really well matched.'

'Just what I've been trying to convince Natalia,' Clay said outrageously, mockery glimmering in his golden eyes.

Liz laughed. 'And I'll bet she told you she didn't have time.' She glanced at Natalia's unresponsive face, then back to Clay. 'She works far too hard,' she said firmly.

Fortunately Mr and Mrs Kaiwhare arrived back then, and the ensuing bustle of introductions silenced Liz.

A little later, however, Natalia—carefully ignoring Clay Beauchamp, still with their group—said half under her breath, 'Stop trying to matchmake.'

'Not interested?' Liz's eyes widened further. 'Truly, Nat?'

'Truly.' Natalia picked up her glass of water with a jerk that almost spilled it.

Liz grinned. 'Then you won't mind if I try my luck, will you?'

The icy water sizzled down Natalia's throat. Meticulously she put the glass down and contemplated the green-skinned wedge of lime decorating its rim. 'Not in the least,' she said tersely, stiffening slightly as she heard Clay laugh.

'Liar,' Liz said cheerfully. 'You're fascinated by each other. Nat, give yourself a break. One rotten apple doesn't mean you have to retire to a nunnery.'

'I haven't got time for romantic entanglements.' Or unromantic ones.

Liz leaned forward, her pretty face vengeful. 'I could throttle Dean Jamieson. He might belong to an old, stiff, rich family with a lot of old, stiff, rich power, but he is a nasty piece of goods. Keeping quiet about his wife, and then spreading it around the district that you tried to break up his marriage was a totally rotten thing to do. Not that it matters—everyone knows he was lying.'

The embarrassment of being warned off only an hour or so previously by yet another wife sprang to Natalia's mind. 'Not everybody,' she said cynically. 'Thanks to his malice, I've now got a reputation.'

'Only with nasty-minded creeps,' Liz said with trenchant, partisan bias. 'They're jealous because you're so stunning and you don't give a cent for the men who try to hit on you.'

Natalia stifled a yelp of laughter. 'You make it sound as though I've cut a swathe through the district!'

'You could if you wanted to.' Liz leaned closer and dropped her voice. 'And you'd better accept that you're as attracted to Clay Beauchamp as he is to you or you're going to find yourself in deep trouble. I suspect he's the bulldozer sort! And as he's living only a mile away—'

Natalia's lip curled. 'He's not a farmer, Liz, he's an agri-businessman, so naturally he lives in Auckland with all the other rich entrepreneurs.'

'Pity,' Liz said pragmatically.

'So no more matchmaking, all right?' Natalia said with emphasis. The band struck up again, a much more modern foxtrot. Gratefully she accepted an invitation from Greg.

'You're looking a bit flushed,' he said, studying her with a professional eye.

'It's hot in here,' she returned. 'You wouldn't think it was the first month of winter, would you? I wonder when it's going to get cold?'

Greg snorted. 'This is north of Auckland—it never gets cold here. In Dunedin it freezes.'

'Poor darling,' she said, primming her mouth. Greg was in his last year at medical school in New Zealand's exquisite southernmost city. Lifting a hand, she patted his cheek. 'I remember the first year you went away, and your parents kept getting anguished faxes about the cold—Liz and I knitted you a jersey each for your birthday, and your mother shipped you off an electric blanket. Did you ever wear those jerseys?'

'Both together, if I remember correctly,' he said with a grin.

Laughing, Natalia looked over his shoulder and met a blaze of gold. Clay Beauchamp was dancing with Liz; as Natalia's brows climbed he deliberately looked away from her and into Liz's small, mischievous face. It felt like a blow.

'…saved my life,' Greg was saying. 'I honestly thought my blood would freeze that first winter.'

Awkwardly she dragged her gaze away from the two striking black and white figures. 'Good,' she said vaguely.

Greg frowned. 'Sure you're all right? You sound a bit disassociated.'

'I'm fine,' she told him crisply.

Within a few moments she'd almost managed to put Clay Beauchamp out of her mind. She and Greg were friends; several years previously he'd fancied himself to be in love with her, only giving up when she told him gently that although she did love him, it was as a brother rather than a lover.

Now they were both satisfied with the way things were between them. When the dance ended, and they were called by friends to the other side of the elegant Victorian ballroom, she went happily with him, staying snug within his arm for the intermission. The next dance was a tango, and she and Greg enjoyed themselves enormously, hamming it up, one of the few couples who dared try it.

Clay Beauchamp, she noticed reluctantly, wasn't dancing; he'd deposited Liz back with the rest of her party and was talking with a group of the major players in the district, including their host.

'Nat, I love showing off with you,' Greg said when it was over and they were the centre of a laughing, clapping group. 'You dance like a dream!' He hugged her extravagantly.

'So, best-beloved, do you.'

Well pleased with each other, they came off arm in arm. Still smiling, Natalia realised that in spite of the disturbing, unsettling, far too intriguing Clay Beauchamp, she was glad she'd come; secure with friends who knew her and loved her she could forget the worry that hung over her like her own private thundercloud.

Back with the rest of their party, she laughed off the compliments and sat down beside Liz, picking up her glass of water. 'Gosh, I enjoy a good tango!'

'You were born to do it,' Liz told her enviously. 'Well, go ahead and ask me.'

'Ask you what?'

'What he said.'

Colour whipped along Natalia's cheekbones. Had she been so obvious? 'I don't know what you mean,' she said haughtily.

Her friend half closed her eyes and pursed her mouth. 'He's far too sophisticated to discuss one woman with another, is Clay Beauchamp. Although I must say I felt him *not* looking at you, if you know what I mean. He was utterly charming. We talked about a lot of things and he didn't lose concentration once, which I thought was pretty clever of him because he just hated seeing you dance with my big brother.'

Natalia put her glass down. 'Liz, don't.'

Her friend's smile disappeared. 'All right, but it's such a *waste*. I hate to go off to England for years and know that once I'm gone you won't let anyone make you go out and have fun. Sometimes I look at your stubborn, tired face and I could kick your father for leaving you in this situation. OK, sermon's over.'

Natalia's eyes stung. 'I have to keep going, Liz.'

Liz opened her mouth, then closed it.

'Yes,' Natalia said with a wry twist to the words, 'his friends were foolish to lend money to him, but you know how persuasive he could be. He really believed he'd make everyone's fortunes with the tunnel-houses.'

'I know. Promise me one thing?'

'What?' Natalia eyed her warily.

'Just have dinner with Mum and Dad once a fortnight, will you? They love having you, and you've cried off their last few invitations.'

'All right,' Natalia said. 'Damn, I'm going to miss you.'

'I'm going to miss you too.'

The band struck up again, and within seconds both were back on the floor. As the evening lengthened, Clay Beauchamp danced with the wives and daughters of the men he'd been speaking to, the district's most solvent and powerful citizens. Bowden wasn't exactly cliquey, but it usually took time for newcomers to be accepted so it was mildly unexpected for him to be welcomed into the fold with such enthusiasm.

Although piqued by his apparent lack of interest, Natalia recognised a ploy as old as time: make your interest known, then pull back to whet the appetite of the person you want.

It was disappointing; she'd expected him to be more subtle.

She set herself to enjoying the rest of the evening, and succeeded so well that the last dance came as an unwelcome surprise. Much more unwelcome was that she found herself in Clay's arms, waltzing.

'Who taught you to dance?' he asked casually.

'My father.'

He nodded. 'He knew what he was doing.'

'Indeed he did.'

'What did I say wrong?'

'Nothing,' she parried. 'Why?'

His eyes were narrowed, the golden fire concentrated and intense. 'He left you in debt, I gather.'

'You *have* been talking,' she said with a false brightness.

That aloof, tilted smile scorched through to her toes. 'And I didn't even have to initiate it. The tango you did with the boyfriend was blatant enough to catch everyone's eye. People were only too eager to talk about you.'

Oh, I'll just bet they were, she thought bitterly. She fought with temptation, but it wasn't fair to embroil Greg in this. 'Greg's a friend—almost a brother—not a boy-friend.'

Dark, straight brows lifted. 'That wasn't what I heard. They were close to taking bets on how long it would take him to get you into bed. Apparently he's been trying for years.'

Grittily, her eyes sparking, she said, 'I'm sorry that men I've known and respected for years should be dirty-minded, lying rumour-mongers.'

Although he laughed, no humour glinted in his eyes. 'It's a human prerogative to be envious of those younger and better-looking, and to wish young women a happy marriage. Especially when the two they're talking about are practically making love on the dance floor.'

'Greg and I were spoofing that tango—as I'm sure every-one else but you realised. And the next time the subject arises,' she said between her teeth, 'you can tell them from me that I have no intention of marrying anyone. If I ever decide to, I'll send a notice to the local newspaper.'

Beneath her hand his shoulder went taut. She felt heat, and a purely male power, and a threat, but his voice was cool and self-contained as he said, 'There won't be a next time. At least not while I'm around.'

'Why?'

He looked over her head, the arrogant features uncompromising. 'Because I indicated that I don't find that sort of speculation interesting.'

'So they just shut up,' she said with sweet cynicism. 'How wonderful to have that sort of authority.'

His smile was formidable. 'You've got an acid tongue. I like that.'

Shrugging, Natalia turned her head away and closed her eyes. Just once—just for a moment—she'd allow herself the illusion that she was safe and protected and in good hands. The green, glittering mask concealed her emotions; no one would know she was listening to the driving beat of Clay's heart, responding helplessly to the strength of his big body against her, breathing in his faint, purely masculine scent.

Neither spoke until the music stopped.

'I'll follow you home,' Clay said as they made their way across the floor.

Natalia bestowed a glittering smile on her old school fellow and his possessive wife. 'That's not necessary, thank you.'

'Possibly not,' Clay agreed with an infuriating inflexibility, 'but I'll do it nevertheless.'

After saying goodbye and thanking her hosts, after arranging a time to get together before Liz left for Oxford, after defiantly accepting Greg's kiss goodnight, Natalia drove her small utility truck carefully away in procession with fifty or so other vehicles. Most of them eventually turned towards Bowden, but one stayed behind her all the way to the intersection of the main highway and the corrugated gravel road that led to her patch of land, and ultimately to Pukekahu.

The dipped lights in her mirror made her jittery. When at last the Xanadu gateway came into view, Natalia put on her indicator and ducked down the drive, glad that she'd left the gate open.

Puddles shone ahead, eerily reflecting the headlights back at her like a series of tiny fallen moons. She knew where the potholes were, but the man who followed her didn't. Hiding a kick of nervousness with a muttered curse, she stopped outside the big shed that acted as a garage.

The car behind stopped; telling herself she was being an idiot, Natalia banged down the lock on the truck door and waited with her hand hovering over the horn, eyes stretched almost painfully as Clay's tall figure unfolded from the car.

Her breath whooshed through suddenly relaxed lips. Quickly she unlocked the door and opened it. 'Why did you follow me in?' she asked, trying to rein in a swift, unusual fury.

'Because I wanted to,' he said caustically, and shocked her by lifting her down.

Alarmed at the strength of the hands that bit into her waist, she grabbed his shoulders to steady herself. Beneath the black cashmere of his dinner jacket she felt muscles curl and flex. He suddenly seemed very large and far too strong. 'Thank you,' she said in a brittle, tense voice.

He settled her on to her feet and let her go. 'I'll go in with you.'

'Thank you again, but I really don't need you to see me to my door.'

'*I* don't see how you're going to stop me.'

Now was the time to finish this once and for all. Trying to sound both patient and composed, she said, 'Clay, I'm sorry if the very light flirtation we indulged in made you hopeful of going to bed with me tonight, but I don't do one-night stands—'

'That "light flirtation",' he interrupted with nerve-tightening self-assurance, 'was a pleasant, mildly exciting preliminary. As you're being so frank, let me tell you that when we make love it won't be a one-night stand. I want you, and I know perfectly well that you want me.'

'How do you know?' she blustered, his blunt statement exploding an unbidden, erotic charge in the pit of her stomach.

Pale light from the hidden moon sifted through the thick cloud pall, revealing the forceful angles and planes of his face. Clay's mouth twisted into a smile; Natalia was already stepping back when he caught her wrist and pulled her against him; still holding her wrist, he bent his head. Unerringly his mouth found hers, shaped it to his own.

Made prisoner by the firmness of his mouth, its warmth, its hunger, Natalia sank into suffocating, humiliating need. Her lips softened, parted slightly in the signal of surrender—and Clay straightened.

'That's how,' he said levelly.

Shame washed the heat and carnality out of her, stiffened her spine, hardened her resolve. 'Clay, I'm not getting involved with you.'

Against the heavy, turbulent sky she saw his head move. Panic warred with exhilaration. More than anything else in the world she wanted him to kiss her again, and that terrified her. She'd never felt like this before, as though everything she'd built her life on was worth nothing without Clay's kisses.

Staring up at him like a terrorised rabbit, she shivered.

'What the hell are we doing sniping at each other in the cold?' he demanded, exasperation sharpening his tone. 'Get inside—it's going to rain any minute.'

Summoning her dignity, Natalia pivoted on her high-heeled sandals and stalked ahead of him through the gate, past the daphne bush her mother had planted and the ghostly heads of the luculia, their scents mingling in a glorious combination of musk and citrus on the damp, cool air.

At the front door she took out the key and turned to say meticulously, 'Thank you for seeing me home.'

'I'll wait here until you've checked the place,' he said inflexibly.

No doubt she should be grateful he didn't insist on doing it himself! Switching on the light inside the door, she marched stiffly down the short hall.

When she returned a few minutes later he was looking out over her small domain; although she'd walked quietly, he swung around before she got to the door.

Natalia's eyes widened. He'd taken off his mask, as had she. His potent male mystery and glamour should have departed with it, but Clay Beauchamp's magnificent bone structure gave him a fierce, elemental beauty that was dramatised dynamic power. Natalia had to keep her hands by her sides to stop them from exploring the thin scar reaching from his jaw to the tip of his right eyebrow.

'I'd expected to be disappointed,' he said, his magnetic gaze raking her face.

She forced her dazed eyes to gaze levelly at him, forced her unwilling mouth into a taunting smile. 'And do you like what you see, now the mask is gone?'

'You lovely witch,' he said, his voice deep and smoky. 'We've a long way to go before all the masks are off. But it's going to happen. Sleep as badly as I'm going to.'

He turned his back on her and walked away. Swallowing to ease an arid throat, Natalie stared after him. He had the ideal male form—triangular torso, long, strong-muscled legs, and that steady pace, lazily menacing as a panther's predatory prowl. At the gate he turned and lifted his hand in a wave that was probably an exercise in sarcasm.

Nerves jumping, she waited until she heard the car start, then slammed the door and stood with her hands clenched until the sound of the engine had died into a silence unlike anything she'd ever experienced.

Shouting meaty, satisfying oaths at the Hereford steer as it ambled carelessly through the teatree and gorse, Natalia dragged black, sticky strands of hair back from her hot face.

'And stay off my property, or I'll kill you for dog tucker,' she finished with vindictive venom, mopping her forehead on the sleeve of her faded T-shirt.

'If you kept your fences in better repair it wouldn't be able to wander.'

The crisp male voice had her whirling around to see Clay Beauchamp dismounting from a horse in one swift, easy movement. Why ride a horse nowadays when farm bikes were a much more efficient way of getting around rural New Zealand? Tall, so big he almost blotted out a couple of tree ferns and a gorse bush, he strode towards her, his angular, autocratic face amused as he looked down his nose at her.

His amusement set tinder to her already explosive temper. Unwisely, she returned, 'Why should I look after your fence? My livestock don't wander.' Fairness compelled her to add, 'And neither do yours, except for this blasted wretch. It keeps breaking in and eating the capsicums. It's smashed through my electric fences more times than I can count.'

The aristocratic amusement vanished; Clay said abruptly, 'A new fence will be up shortly.'

'Good. Until then, keep that damn steer off my land or I'll shoot it,' Natalia snapped.

Furious with herself for losing control, she turned to make her way across the small swamp that marked the boundary between Xanadu and Pukekahu. Sweat blinded her, sweat and anger and frustration. The steer had pushed its way into a tunnel-house and that long pink tongue had ruined too many plants.

But, however angry she'd been, she shouldn't have shouted at Clay. It wasn't his fault that one steer had damaged the tunnel-house—and she certainly couldn't blame him for the state of the boundary fence, because it was Dean Jamieson who'd systematically stripped Pukekahu of every asset and refused to spend a cent on the station.

She'd made an idiot of herself.

An insect came barrelling at her, a tiny, threatening missile in the sunshine. Dread kicked in her stomach; she leaped sideways, landed in muddy water with one ankle twisted beneath her, and fell on to her knees with a yelp as pain pierced the skin of her bare arm.

'What the hell is the matter with you?' Hands wrenched her to her feet, jerked her out of the water and hauled her across to dry land. Setting her on her feet, Clay demanded harshly, 'What is it?'

'Only a bee-sting,' she gasped, looking at the poison sac left in her arm. He moved, she thought dazedly, very fast for such a big man.

'You're allergic to them?'

'No.' She dragged in a deep breath and squared her shoulders, forced herself to meet frowning tawny-gold eyes. 'I'm allergic to wasps,' she said succinctly. 'That's what I thought the bee was—and when it stung me I realised I'd come without my pills.'

Before she'd finished speaking Clay had taken a pocket knife from his hip pocket and opened it. She barely had time to register the cold steel sliding along her heated skin before he'd flicked the poison sac free. Another movement, and she watched, shivering, as the blade was folded back, the knife returned to its place.

'Careless of you, wasn't it?' Clay said pleasantly, black brows lifting.

Natalia had as little liking as anyone for being called foolish, but he was right. In early winter most wasps were slow and easily seen, but the newly mated queens could be aggressive. She'd been lucky this time; normally she wouldn't have set foot outside the house without her pills.

'Very,' she said coolly. 'But I was too busy getting rid of the steer trashing the tunnel-house to think about wasps.'

Eyes the golden-brown of topaz examined her, travelling from her tangle of curls to her wide, green eyes, and then on to her mouth. His smile acknowledged ivory skin and soft red lips, the female desirability of a body honed by hard work.

It was a purely sexual appraisal, and it was done with every intention to intimidate. Natalia's skin tightened as more adrenaline surged through her bloodstream, quickening her breath. I don't need this, she thought savagely, stepping away.

'Thank you for picking me up,' she said in aloof dismissal. 'I'll be all right now.'

'You don't want a ride home?'

Natalia glanced at the patiently waiting horse. Mellow sunlight washed over its black hide. Had Clay chosen the horse to go with his hair?

'No, thank you,' she said, and turned her back on man and horse. Stiff-spined, she walked up the hill, bristling under that golden predatory scrutiny until she reached sanctuary in the native bush cloaking the hillside.

Only then did she relax, her breath whistling out between dry lips. If he'd slept as badly as she had, he'd have been sluggish too. Instead, he'd shown her up as a clumsy, forgetful idiot. Why did he have to buy the place next door? It infuriated her that she was totally unable to deal with a man who exuded sex and authority from every pore of that big, lithe, graceful body.

OK, so she'd responded to it. And, yes, her nostrils still quivered at the faint male scent she'd registered when he'd carried her across the swamp, and her skin felt oddly tender where he'd grabbed her.

However, she knew how little it meant. A mixture of attractive packaging and pheromones—abetted by some elemental treachery in the female psyche—had stirred her hormones, but she wasn't going to surrender to them again. Dean Jamieson had taught her a lesson she wouldn't forget—she was no more immune to masculine charisma than any other woman of twenty-three.

However, she had more pressing things to do than worry

about Clay Beauchamp. Fixing the gap in the electric fence, for one.

It turned out to be one of those days. While the steer had been satisfying its appetite for capsicums it had smashed a vital piece of the hydroponic watering system. Not only that—until she could afford to replace the broken piece, Natalia would have to get up every two hours during the night to check the tunnel-house.

She toyed with the idea of billing Clay Beauchamp; the only thing that stopped her was that he would be entirely within his rights to demand that she pay half the cost of fixing the boundary fence.

Her afternoon was cheered by a phone call from the local supermarket, asking for a couple of boxes of peppers. Whistling, she went out to pick and pack them, then headed off down the road in the truck.

Before she'd got off the gravel road an explosion like a rifle-shot and a sudden vicious yank on the steering wheel sent adrenaline pumping through her. Battling with the wheel, she managed to wrestle the runaway vehicle on to the grass verge and kill the engine.

'What else?' she muttered as she got out, hiding her desperation with a ferocious frown.

Everything had been going so well until—until Clay Beauchamp arrived on the scene. He was turning out to be a bad luck charm. It figured, she thought sourly. Clay—what a ridiculous name! It was probably short for Clayton, only he didn't look like a Clayton. He fitted Clay—or it fitted him; in spite of that worldly gloss he was elemental, earthy, primally male.

She knelt by the offending tyre, wincing at the strips of rubber shredded from it. Beyond prayer. Gravel bit into her knee; she got to her feet and brushed down her threadbare jeans.

Of course the spare wheel didn't want to come out, and it was filthy. Pressing her lips together, Natalia tugged it free, coughing in the cloud of clinging road dust that accompanied it.

The sound of an engine coming fast made her start; infuriatingly, because normally she wasn't clumsy, the wheel escaped through her hands and bounced on to the road too close to her feet. After an involuntary leap backwards she snatched at it, but had to watch helplessly as it rolled across the road towards the big burgundy car swinging around the corner.

CHAPTER THREE

CLAY applied the brakes, skilfully controlled the subsequent skid as the car fishtailed, then brought the vehicle to a halt just as the spare wheel hurtled into the driver's door with jarring, bone-chilling noise. Watching it bounce off, Natalia felt sick.

The burgundy door opened and Clay emerged in a lethal, silent rush. As the wheel spun across the road and eventually fell, he demanded in a deep, raw voice, 'What the hell is going on?'

'I'm sorry—I dropped my spare wheel,' Natalia told him crisply. Or as crisply as she could when her stomach was jumping like a just-caught marlin.

Clay's mouth curved. 'Really? Or did you throw it?' he asked, his slow drawl a contrast to the swift assessment in his glance.

Stung, she said, 'No. I don't destroy things.'

He turned back to eye the dented and scratched paintwork of his indecently opulent BMW. Its value would probably wipe off her mortgage and leave some left over, she thought with a hard, rebellious defiance.

Envy was a lousy emotion, especially when it was mixed with self-pity, so she banished it.

'My door doesn't exactly look whole,' he observed.

Natalia bit her lip. 'It was an accident. I really am sorry. As you can see, I had a blow-out.'

'I heard it, and thought some fool was shooting.' He looked past her. 'We'd better see whether your spare wheel came off better than my door.'

It hadn't. Natalia stared down at what had been a reasonably good—if filthy—wheel, and the panic that had been building inside her surged to full, shattering fruition.

Clay indicated several dents and a split in the tyre. 'You need a new one.'

She couldn't afford a new one. Angling her chin, she lifted her eyes, only to feel something unnerving slither the length of her spine. He was looking at her with coolly acquisitive pleasure. Although his eyes were the same colour as topaz, they lacked the glitter of gems; instead the gleaming gold was speculative, almost lazy with the knowledge of strength and mastery. As her skin tightened, Natalia thought of lions, relaxed, indolent, deadly.

He said, 'I'll move my car off the road.'

A breeze swooped down from the hills, tossing a curl on to Natalia's cheek. Her skin burned as she pushed the hair back with a shaking hand and watched him stride across the road.

Clay Beauchamp was just too much. The way he moved, the compelling aura around him, his very size—all reinforced the autocratic, controlled authority of his handsome face. How could she dislike him, yet be held captive by such a blind, unwilling fascination?

Seething at whatever malignant fate had tossed this series of disasters her way, she walked back to her truck and glowered at the burst tyre while Clay moved his car on to the grass. She didn't turn as he came up behind her, and he made no noise, but she felt his presence like a shadow on her soul.

'We'd better put those peppers into my boot,' he said, 'and I'll take you wherever you want to deliver them.'

How she wished she could say loftily, Don't bother, I can cope. But she couldn't. The supermarket sourced most of its fruit and vegetables from the markets in Auckland; they used her because she was absolutely reliable and cheap. Glancing at her watch, she said unevenly, 'I'm going to the supermarket, thank you.'

'Do you want to take the wheel off the truck? The garage might have a tyre that will fit it.'

'No, I'll do that later—the supermarket wants the peppers now.'

'All right. Lock up if you think it's necessary. I'll take the peppers across.'

She was behaving badly. It wasn't Clay's fault her tyre had burst, and he had offered her a lift. He had every right to be angry about the ding on his door, yet he hadn't said anything.

Only what to him was a nuisance was for her a major setback. Not only did she have to buy an irrigation valve, but two new tyres and replace the buckled spare wheel. And the rates were due soon, not to mention the power and the phone bill...

And always—*always* her father's debt.

At least her vegetable garden was flourishing, she thought mordantly, watching Clay put the boxes into the car boot. He'd rolled up the sleeves of his shirt; when she saw how easily he picked up the spare wheel and put it in beside the capsicums something coiled within her, coiled lazily and slowly, and stretched, and flexed its claws...

Enough of that, she told herself sternly, and locked the truck before walking reluctantly across to his car.

'Get in, Red Riding Hood,' Clay Beauchamp commanded mockingly.

Her eyes narrowed. 'Why Red Riding Hood?'

His rakish, too perceptive grin told her he'd seen her looking at him. 'Because you're accepting a ride with the wolf?' he said, enough of a taunt in his tone to lift the hairs on her skin.

Natalia had no answer to that, so she took refuge in a shrug. 'I'm more like the Wicked Witch of the West,' she muttered, sliding into the front seat, glad of the mud clinging to the soles of her boots, glad that her jeans showed signs of contact with the road and the spare wheel. Let his expensive car learn what honest dirt was.

'Where's the supermarket?' he asked as he turned the engine on.

It purred, and so, Natalia thought wearily, would any woman who felt his hands on her. Lean, competent, they looked vastly experienced, as though no place on a woman's tender body would be safe from them—or immune. As she gave him directions that hidden hunger inside her stirred again, a repressed sweetness, slow as run honey, powerful and smooth as the best brandy, aching through her.

Why was she so susceptible to handsome men? Her high school boyfriend had been the best-looking boy in the district, and her physical response to Dean Jamieson had lured her close enough to be intrigued by his charm.

But her luck had held—just. Her heart had still been intact when she'd found out about his wife, and she'd turned her back on what could have turned into a messy, sordid affair. She'd emerged with her pride and her independence tarnished, but still intact.

So it was doubly ironic that the only other man who'd made an impression on her since then had also made a large dent in her pride—and was now threatening her independence.

Clay drew into the car park at the supermarket, and insisted on carrying the boxes of peppers inside.

'I can do it,' Natalia said, trying not to sound unappreciative. 'They're not heavy.'

'It's all right; I'm stronger than I look.'

Stressed, she walked beside him into the shop. 'Thanks, Nat,' the woman who ran the produce department said. She cast an appraising glance at Clay and smiled with genuine, startled admiration. 'Just put them here, will you? The usual payment?'

'Yes, that's fine.'

Back at the car, Clay said, 'I hope you get market prices. That's good stuff you have there.'

Natalia said politely, 'We have an arrangement that works well for both of us.'

The wide, arrogant mouth compressed a moment, then relaxed into a smile that almost seduced her into an answering one. Oh, he knew exactly what effect he had on a woman!

And why shouldn't he? Clay Beauchamp probably had to chase glamorous women out of his wardrobe.

He said, 'Where's the garage?'

When they arrived he reached for the ruined spare wheel.

'It's dirty,' Natalia said.

'So?' His voice had an edge to it. 'I know what dirt is.'

She didn't answer. He leaned down to say, 'You're beginning to exasperate me, Natalia.'

She lifted her brows. 'Then I'd better be quiet,' she said dulcetly, 'at least until I get home.'

His brows met in a formidable frown. 'I wouldn't leave you stuck here,' he said shortly as he straightened, and hefted the tyre effortlessly into the shop.

'Hi, Nat,' the man who came out from behind the counter said. 'Did you have a good time last night?'

'Wonderful, thanks, Mr Stephens. Can you order me a tyre for this wheel?'

Mr Stephens looked at it. 'It's buckled,' he pointed out unnecessarily. 'Do you want another wheel too?'

'No, I'll send the good wheel in to you on Monday so you can fit the new tyre.' In spite of her attempt to sound her normal cheerful self, her words emerged clipped; Clay's silent presence tugged at her nerves like a comb over wool.

Mr Stephens looked at Clay. To Natalia's outrage Clay gave a short nod; relieved, the older man turned to her and said, 'All right, then. I'll put it on the rural delivery on Tuesday.'

Clay said nothing until they were back in the car. Then, as he turned the key to start it, he said, 'All your tyres are shot—they're dangerous, and even if another doesn't blow out, you're not going to get a warrant of fitness next time you take the truck in.'

Colourlessly Natalia said, 'Quite possibly. I'll contact my

insurance company on Monday—no doubt they'll be in touch with you soon afterwards. I'm really sorry about the door.'

His low laugh had a savage note in it. 'I understand pride—sometimes it's been the only thing that's kept me going. I presume you can't afford to pay for a new wheel.'

'You presume too much,' she said frostily.

There was a moment's taut silence. Then he said quietly, 'Point taken. We need to talk about fences. Boundary fences, to be specific.'

That was when Natalia remembered she'd be liable for half the cost of any new boundary fence between Xanadu and Pukekahu Station. She drew in a quick, jolting breath and tried to relax shoulders aching with sudden strain. 'Yes, of course.'

He said, 'Come up to dinner tomorrow night. How does seven o'clock sound?'

With rigid precision she said, 'I'd rather discuss business more formally.'

In a tone that nudged too close to contempt, he said, 'I don't discuss business at social occasions. However, if you feel so strongly, come to the office at the homestead at three o'clock tomorrow afternoon.'

Which left her with nothing to say but, 'Yes, all right.'

He nodded. Biting back hot, unwise words, Natalia sat in tense silence that lasted until they drove past the truck.

Clay asked laconically, 'What are you going to do about that?'

'It'll be OK here,' she said, hoping she was right. 'It's well off the road, so a driver would have to try hard to hit it.'

A stray beam of sun outlined his forceful profile, reinforcing the arrogant cut of his jaw and the symmetrical, autocratic bone structure as he nodded. Natalia looked straight ahead, her expression held under stony discipline.

When he drove into her gateway she said steadily, 'You

can put me down here, thank you.' The last thing she wanted was for him to see inside her home.

'You'll get wet before you're halfway there—it's trying to rain.'

Sure enough, one of early winter's soft showers was gathering around the ridges, ready to billow down the hills and across the narrow coastal flats to lose itself in the wide expanse of the Pacific Ocean.

'Rain won't melt me,' Natalia said, hiding her defensiveness with unemphatic words and a flat tone.

'So you're a tough, hard woman.' The drawled comment was meant to be sarcastic, and succeeded. 'Why are you so prickly, Natalia?'

'I have no idea what you mean,' she said, each word so clearly articulated it could have sliced through ice. As the car drew up outside the ramshackle shed that was both garage and packhouse, she unclipped her seat belt.

His eyes narrowed and his mouth tilted into a mirthless smile, his keen gaze lingering on her hot cheeks. A feverish shiver pulled her skin tight.

'Your eyes fire up brilliantly when you're angry,' he said, the words smooth and taunting.

'Whereas you become offensive.' She should be intimidated but she wasn't; adrenaline pumped through her in a singing, exhilarating flood.

'What makes you think I'm angry? This offensiveness could be my normal attitude.'

'I'm giving you the benefit of the doubt,' she retorted sweetly.

Swift as a striking bird of prey, Clay caught her tense hand and kissed the palm. Lean, tanned fingers tightened around her wrist; Natalia felt their controlled power like a fetter. Then he released her.

As she snatched back her hand Natalia thought she could feel the sensuous touch of his lips still burning on her skin.

'Don't dare me,' he said evenly, his eyes dwelling on the soft curves of her breasts for a heart-stopping second before lifting to trap her gaze. Heat lit the tawny depths to gold, yet she couldn't see emotion there, nothing but an intense, primal hunger.

'How interesting your life must be—full of dares and challenges unrecognised by other people,' she retorted in a brittle voice. 'If I ever dare you, I'll do it deliberately. And this isn't a dare, either—I don't want to flirt with you, or be the recipient of your approaches.'

'You have a charming, old-fashioned turn of phrase,' he said, mockery quirking the corners of that beautifully cut mouth, so chiselled that its strength wasn't immediately noticeable. 'Is that a heritage from your mother? I believe she was Russian.'

Liz must have told him.

Willing her pulses to slow down, Natalia drew in a swift breath. That kiss had been meant as a small punishment, and by overreacting she'd reinforced it. Pride transformed her embarrassment into a stony inflection. 'My mother was born in New Zealand, but her parents were Russian refugees who'd learned their English from Victorian novels. She spoke more formally than most New Zealanders, so possibly I inherited it. And now,' she said idiotically, 'I have to go. Thank you for your kindness.'

She scrabbled behind her for the door handle and jerked it open, intent only on getting out of there.

The window on the passenger's side of the car wound magically down. He said, 'I'll pick you up tomorrow afternoon.'

'No, thank you,' she said evenly, and when he frowned added curtly, 'I prefer to walk.'

He gave her a long, considering stare, followed by an abrupt nod. The window wound up and the car drew away.

Natalia stepped back against the gate, leaning on it until the big car had disappeared. 'Damn,' she whispered. 'Oh, damn.'

And turned into the house, walking up the path, barely

noticing the burgeoning spires of redhot pokers or the last apricot trumpets of the datura.

Kicking off her boots in the laundry, she tried to estimate how much her half of a new boundary fence would cost; added to the other outgoings she'd racked up over the past couple of days, it came to an appalling amount of money.

'Oh, Dad,' she whispered, resting her forehead against the cool glass of the window. 'You really left me in a mess, didn't you?'

Twenty-four hours later, as she walked up to Pukekahu, Natalia was still worrying. But because she'd spent most of her waking hours trying to decide which clothes to wear for this interview, she was disgusted with herself.

In the end she'd settled on an elderly pair of black trousers that made the most of her long legs, and a poplin shirt the same green as her eyes. For luck she'd twisted around her wrist a thin gold chain her grandmother had given her. Because it wasn't worth much it was the only thing she'd kept. Possibly the chain was a little dramatic for a business interview, but with any luck Clay would put it down to her Russian blood.

It took her fifteen minutes to walk through the cloudy afternoon to Pukekahu; as she approached the homestead Natalia sped up, hoping that the heavy clouds on the horizon stayed there.

Once Pukekahu homestead had been a glorious Victorian villa set in luxuriant subtropical gardens, but years of neglect had transformed the huge wooden building into a ruin, and the garden to a wild, overgrown tangle.

Natalia looked around. Although old Mr Freeman had let the place run down, it had been Dean Jamieson who'd allowed it to disintegrate. He'd told her he simply didn't have enough money—and because she'd been temporarily infatuated she'd tried to believe him. No doubt the station had been a bargain for Clay, although it would cost a huge amount of money to make the house livable again.

Where was the office? She hesitated at the foot of a wide, high set of stairs that led up on to a wooden verandah, its balustrade entwined with clinging loops of jasmine, the red buds already opening to white flowers that exuded a scent almost cloying in its musky intensity.

Setting her mouth firmly, she began to climb the steps. At the top she headed towards an open door. As her feet clattered over the long unpainted boards Clay appeared in the doorway.

Natalia's unwilling gaze was snared by a sudden blaze of gold. It vanished immediately, hidden by the fringe of his lashes as he said her name.

Swiftly, gripped by a chill of foreboding, she said, 'It's a pity the garden's so overgrown. It has some stunning trees in it.'

'Most of them are dying,' he said smoothly. 'Come in.'

Once inside she looked around and said, 'Oh!'

'What did you expect—ruins and dampness, decay and degradation?' An undertone in his voice flicked across her nerves.

'Well—you have to admit the outside looks pretty dilapidated!'

In front of her stretched an oriental carpet, its rich copper and blue hues subtly interwoven, and beyond it flames jumped in an embellished Victorian fireplace. Comfortable modern furniture picked up the paler colours in the rug, and a huge desk was set up with what was surely the latest in computer equipment.

Clay had taken over one of the sitting rooms for his office, and had clearly been in residence for some time.

'Sit down,' he said. 'It's not really cold enough for a fire, but it always looks welcoming.'

'It's lovely,' Natalia said, studiously keeping her eyes averted from his handsome, authoritative face. 'I hadn't realised the house had been renovated.'

'It hasn't. This is the only livable room in it, and the engineer I commissioned to see if it was worth saving warned me it could easily collapse under me. In fact, it's probably only held together by the jasmine.'

Natalia sat down. To fill the silence she remarked, 'I was surprised to hear that Pukekahu had been sold. And no one knew who had bought it—you kept things very quiet.'

'I don't make a habit of talking about my business affairs,' he said smoothly. 'Didn't Phil tell you he had a new boss?'

'I haven't seen him much lately,' Natalia responded, too aware of those leonine eyes on her face. Phil had taken her refusal to go out with him again badly; in the end she'd told him as gently as she could not to contact her again. Hastily she asked, 'What are you going to do with it?'

'The homestead? It will have to be demolished; so will that hovel Phil's living in. I'll build a decent manager's house. And then I'll set about turning the station into a productive unit.' He spoke tersely, a thread of steel running through his voice.

What would it be like to have that sort of money? Natalia looked down at her hands, the fingernails short and unpolished, still showing—in spite of hearty scrubbing—signs of her day's work.

'Can I get you some tea?' Clay asked. 'Or coffee?'

Natalia looked up, her eyes widening as they met the challenge in his. Dry-mouthed, she said, 'I'd rather talk about the boundary fence.'

Something about Clay tugged at her senses and scrambled her brain. She needed a clear head, and she needed to get out of here.

'I've done a costing of the fence between Xanadu and Pukekahu,' he said calmly, walking across to the desk and picking up a sheet of paper. 'You'd better have a look at it.'

Wishing she'd had the sense to remain standing, Natalia took the paper and stared at the figures. Bold, black numbers wavered before her eyes; she blinked surreptitiously and concentrated on adding them up.

It came to less than her estimate, but not much.

Holding herself very still, she said, 'I can't afford to pay half of this. Furthermore, I don't really need a fence—I keep my animals in with an electric one. However, I'll put it up if you provide the materials.' She tried to sound matter-of-fact, impersonal, but the words emerged flat and defensive.

Black brows drew into a formidable frown. 'Can you?' he asked, not attempting to hide his scepticism.

Her smile was spiced with a fierce enjoyment. 'Oh, yes,' she said lightly, handing back the sheet of paper. 'My skills might be unsophisticated, but they are useful.'

His eyes never left her face. Not a muscle moved in the big, poised body—the sheet of paper in his hand stayed steady. Primitive instinct locked Natalia in stasis. She didn't even breathe until he said indifferently, 'Forget about the fence—it doesn't matter.'

Natalia's head lifted. 'I pay my way.'

'I don't prey on the poor,' he interrupted, a swift, brutal irritation edging his voice. 'Pukekahu doesn't need any sacrifice from you.'

Her skin felt clammy as heat seeped from it, to be replaced by a fierce tide of colour when humiliation hit home.

Before she could speak he said with a cool smile, 'If it will appease your pride, I'll make a condition.'

'What?' she asked, suspicion hiding her dread.

Aware of her thoughts, he smiled narrowly. 'No, I don't have to bribe or blackmail women into my bed,' he said with a silky tinge of menace. 'But if you ever want to sell your place, come to me first.'

'Of course,' she said stiffly. 'Do you want me to sign something?'

When he hesitated, honesty compelled an admission; forcing the words between reluctant lips, she added, 'Not that I'll sell Xanadu.'

His eyes quizzed her. '"*In Xanadu did Kubla Khan a stately pleasure-dome decree,*"' he quoted. 'That Xanadu?'

No doubt he was laughing at the idea that the small, neglected house she lived in, with its pervading smell of damp, could represent anyone's idea of paradise. 'That's the one,' Natalia said, using cynicism to conceal her raw pride. 'My father was a dreamer, you see.'

'The children of dreamers usually turn out to be severely practical.'

He was pushing, but she wasn't going to give. Getting to her feet, she said in a hard, emotionless voice, 'I have to go.'

Rain pelted suddenly down on the iron roof, invading the room with thunder. After a hooded scrutiny of her face, Clay walked across to the door and looked out, almost filling the opening. In spite of her bitter shame, something stirred deep inside Natalia, something treacherous and hungry.

'How old are you?' he asked abruptly.

Startled, she told him.

'You don't look twenty-three.' Golden eyes scanned her face, assessing her in a dauntingly impersonal survey that lifted her hackles. After a moment he said quietly, 'Perhaps you do—it's your confidence that makes you seem more mature than most women of your age.'

'Thanks,' she said. 'How old are you?'

'Thirty.'

'It must be that confidence thing again. I'd put you as a few years older.'

He grinned. *'Touché,'* he said softly, somehow making the fencer's acknowledgment of a hit an intimate, teasing observation.

Astonished, Natalia's lashes dropped. His face hardened and he said, 'I'll take you home. This rain isn't going to stop in a hurry.' He smiled without humour. 'Unless you'd like to stay here until it does.'

A reluctant, feverish excitement leapt across her nerve-ends. It was humiliating and she hated it. Pasting a smile to her face, she said brightly, 'Thank you, but I have things to do.' Capsicums to pick and pack, cattle to move, hens to feed and shut up.

Something of her turbulent emotions must have shown in her face because his mouth curved in another brief, ironic smile. 'Now that I think of it, you could do me a favour.'

CHAPTER FOUR

DISDAIN curled through Natalia's voice and iced her eyes, hiding, she hoped, the savage thrust of disappointment. A stupid disappointment, because there was nothing but powerful sexual attraction between them. 'On my back? I thought you said you weren't interested? Forget it—I'm not that desperate. Or that poor.'

'You,' Clay said pleasantly, 'have either a dirty mind or a mercenary one. If you think sex is merely a favour, you are, of course, entitled to your opinion. However, just to set the record straight, I don't ask for sex in return for favours. And when we make love there'll be no question of payment.'

'There's no question of mak…making…of anything,' she flared, both angered and excited by his calm assumption that it was going to happen. 'I told you, half an hour of light flirtation at a masquerade ball is no basis on which to build a relationship.' With cutting finality, she ended, 'Any sort of relationship, even the most basic one of satisfying an itch.'

His black brows shot up. 'And you're making sure there's nothing else to build it on. I've never seen anyone back-pedal so fast. Been burned, Natalia?'

'Who hasn't?'

'Not over it yet?'

She gave him a smouldering, defiant stare. 'Of course I am—not that there was much to get over!'

'It's odd, then, that your reaction is so explosive.' With one stride he invaded her comfort zone, his fingers insultingly possessive as they found the hammering pulse at her wrist.

55

'The signs of temper are almost the same as arousal,' he murmured, regarding her with calculating eyes. 'Your eyes are green and glittering, and that pretty flush along those elegant cheekbones could be anger. But angry people tighten their lips…and yours are soft and full.' He lifted her wrist to his mouth.

Desperately Natalia tried to make a fist, tried to remember the moves taught in the self-defence course she'd taken years ago, but her bones had no stuffing and she couldn't move.

Although his mouth was gentle on her skin, what brought a harsh little sound breaking past her closed throat was the tip of his tongue tracing the palm with erotic finesse. His lashes had drooped; a dusky colour stained his skin.

Yes, she thought exultantly, oh, yes…

Still with her hand against his mouth, he said, 'So we've established that it's not temper—or not entirely.'

He looked at her, and she flinched at the triumph blazing in his narrowed eyes. 'You should see yourself,' he said silkily. 'Heavy eyelids and a lush mouth, skin as fine and translucent as the most precious ivory, your lithe, graceful body curving towards me—you promise all the delights that poor old Kubla Khan wanted in his Xanadu.'

Branded, marked on her soul by the moment his mouth had touched her and drained her of stamina, of resolve, of autonomy, Natalia jerked her arm back convulsively. He let her go with a casual dismissiveness, watching as she rubbed her wrist against her thigh.

'Life would be infinitely more simple if you could get rid of desire so easily,' he said cynically. 'Stop that, you'll rub your skin raw.'

'Damn you, I'm not delicate or weak,' she said, her voice uneven and blurred, her arms stiff at her sides. 'I'm strong.'

'And I find the prospect of your strength infinitely seductive,' he said coolly. Before she could answer, he added, 'If you have a prejudice against making love on your back, I'd be delighted to introduce you to other, more adventurous positions.'

For a single extravagant, treacherous second she saw him lying beneath her, sprawled like an indolent cat, his golden skin gleaming in the light of lamps. The image lingered suffocatingly in her mind as she said on an impeded note, 'Forget it.'

He shrugged. 'I wish I could.' Although heat still lingered in his golden eyes, his voice became cool, controlled. 'To go back to your original misapprehension, I want to host a party to repay my social obligations at a restaurant in Bowden. I need a hostess. If you do that we'll be even— and you can forget about the fence.'

She almost said yes. The word trembled on her tongue, but when she saw the flash of calculation in his smile she knew what he'd been trying to do. It hurt that he should think she was so easily conned. 'I'm not a charity case— you don't have to think up false jobs so you can drop a few cents in my hand.' Scorn vibrated in her voice. 'If you really need a hostess, get someone older. If I do it, people will put the worst construction on it.'

'The worst? That I'm blackmailing you—forcing you to act as hostess at a dinner party?' His irony flicked her pride.

'That we are lovers,' she said with cold bluntness. A fierce, perverse satisfaction gripped her when anger gleamed behind his thick lashes.

Leashing it, he said uncompromisingly, 'They'll only be a bit in advance of reality.'

The fire crackled suddenly, sending warm light flaming across his autocratic face to highlight the hawkish good looks, the powerful framework that would make him striking until the day he died. Swift, unwanted sensation melted Natalia's spine and fogged her brain, robbing her of the ability to think.

Apparently taking her silence for acquiescence, he glanced at the rain, still hosing down. 'You've already established your independence, so don't insist on walking home in this. I'll take you.'

Although he spoke perfectly pleasantly, a faint threat underlined his words. If she pushed too far he looked willing to pick her up and dump her into his car.

He could try.

Rigidly she said, 'I don't cut off my nose to spite my face. Thank you.'

Stifling an angry, forbidden excitement, Natalia strode beside him to the back of the house, where he unfurled a vast, brilliantly coloured golf umbrella. 'Come on,' he said tersely.

Rain hurled down in solid sheets. If she'd insisted on walking home she'd have been soaked immediately. At first Natalia tried to keep as far from Clay as she could, but after two steps he said caustically, 'It won't poison you if you put your hand on my arm and walk in step with me.'

Reluctantly she did that, telling herself that she could not feel the throb of his life force through her fingertips, however sensitised they were. Walking beside him in a small column of dryness with the smell of rain in her nostrils was a powerfully intimate experience; she felt both protected and challenged, and was relieved when at last they got to the big implement shed.

As Clay shook water off the umbrella just inside the wide door, a man looked up from a long bench where he'd been working on a piece of machinery.

'Nat!' he exclaimed, his face lighting up. His glance swung to the man beside her, and after a pause he added in a flat voice, 'Clay.'

Warily conscious of Clay beside her, Natalia responded, 'Hi, Phil. How are things?' She moved away from Clay, very conscious of his alert interest.

Phil's eyes devoured her. 'Great. Things are great.'

'Good.' She smiled at him, silently thanking Clay when he asked about the machinery that Phil was working on. The two men spoke for a few moments until Clay said,

'We'd better get going. I'll see you in ten minutes or so, Phil.'

Phil slid another look at Natalia. 'OK. See you later, Nat,' he said, and turned back to the bench.

Clay's huge car smelt of money, Natalia thought dispassionately as she did up her seat belt—money and freedom.

Halfway down the drive Clay asked calmly, as though he had a right to know, 'When did you two stop being lovers?'

Rage and shame fired a lethal cocktail into her bloodstream. She toyed with the idea of telling him it was no business of his, but he had only to ask someone in the district to find out. 'Phil and I went out together until about two months ago. We broke up amicably.'

On her part, anyway.

'About the time I bought Pukekahu,' Clay said.

Natalia shrugged. 'I didn't know that.'

'You might have dumped him amicably,' Clay drawled, 'but he's still eating you with his eyes, poor devil.'

She masked the sudden leap of her nerves with an enquiring stare. Nothing in Clay's tone should have made her wary, yet it took will-power to say, 'Now *you're* suffering from a misapprehension.'

Clay shifted the gear lever down, his mouth curving. 'Barely adult, yet already a *femme fatale*.' His voice was coolly reflective, his eyes narrowed to reveal only a sliver of gold.

'What a quaint, old-fashioned term,' she said with relish. 'I suppose your parents were New Zealanders, so you can't even blame it on a foreign heritage. Do you read historical novels? Nowadays such women are called nymphomaniacs or cold bitches. I'm certainly not the first, and I don't think I'm a cold bitch, either.'

'Then why the lack of concern in your voice? And the dismissive body language? You were superficially friendly, but you couldn't have made your rejection more obvious.'

She said steadily, 'Encouragement would have been more cruel.'

After a short silence Clay said with soft menace, 'He'll be working on the fence, so keep away. If you're not going to give the poor devil what he craves, don't torment him.'

Natalia leashed her temper. 'I'm not into torment,' she said woodenly. Clay had just made it impossible for her to help with the boundary fence.

Was that the reason he'd told her Phil would be putting up the fence—so that she'd stay clear? A quick, angry glance at his angular profile defused that idea. Hardly; if he considered her to be a *femme fatale* he probably thought she'd be down there at every available moment tantalising poor Phil.

Ahead gaped the shed at Xanadu, an empty space where the truck usually stood. Clay nosed the big car inside.

When Natalia went to get out he said, 'Here,' and handed her a blank signed cheque. 'Fill in the cost of any damage the heifer did,' he said, his unhurried self-possession reinforcing her resistance.

Temptation wooed her.

Before she could speak, he said with an amused cynicism, 'Don't be prissy, Natalia.'

She dropped the cheque. 'I'll get a quote and let you know what the amount is,' she retorted.

Not looking at him, she unclipped the seat belt. From the corner of her eye she saw him move, and her head whipped around. 'What are you doing?'

On a note of savage irony he snapped, 'I left my umbrella in the shed; I'm coming in with you.'

He didn't seem to be the sort of man who'd forget things. Did she scramble his brain as much as he did hers? It was a disturbing, exciting thought, one she pondered as she climbed out and turned to face him with an arrogantly tilted chin.

Rain drove on to the rusty corrugated iron roof, deafening her, but she said loudly, 'I'm capable of getting to the house without your help.'

'I know,' he said, his eyes gleaming, 'but sometimes I like to live dangerously. Let's go.'

Scooping her in front of him, so that his broad shoulders and height sheltered her from the driving rain, he growled, 'Run,' and propelled her forward.

He smelt of rain, Natalia thought, responding with a visceral immediacy to his male scent, its very faintness at odds with its potent effect on her. Heat enveloped her as he matched his long strides to her shorter ones, both of them moving with an ease and physical understanding that bypassed awkwardness and catapulted her into a forbidden intimacy.

Clay Beauchamp was a stranger—one she disliked and didn't trust—yet with each step a fierce, unwanted urgency stripped layers of common sense and logic and prudence from her.

The back door promised deliverance. 'Here we are,' she said tightly when they were at last under the narrow porch. Turning, she added reluctantly, 'Thank you.'

She found herself looking up into his face, stark, formidable, into tawny eyes smouldering with the same violent hunger that racked her.

'Natalia,' he said, as though it was a curse, and then he kissed her, and the fire she'd been banking down—the white-hot intensity she'd renounced—burst into a conflagration and consumed her.

His mouth was hard, demanding far more from her than she was prepared to give. But, oh, she was bewitched! Hunger clawed through her, offering all the forbidden glory of passion, all the sweets of heaven—if she would only surrender.

Her arms locked around his shoulders, outstretched fingers clinging to the powerful muscles beneath the thin, damp material of his shirt. Drugged, reft away into a dark enchantment of the senses, Natalia fought a battle with the famished, mindless need that had sprung into such terrifying, wild life.

Stop, she whimpered silently, stop! Now. *Stop*.

Clay's chest expanded, dragging her shirt exquisitely over her sensitive nipples. Against her lips he asked harshly, 'Did I hurt you?'

'No.' Her voice sounded husky, absent. She forced her seeking hands away from his shoulders, bracing herself to step back from the heat and strength of his big body.

He kissed the corner of her mouth before moving with delicious precision to the lobe of her ear. His teeth bit into the soft skin, and sensation shot through her like lightning—jagged, all-consuming, destructive, and ferociously beautiful.

This is Clay Beauchamp, her mind managed to insist, in spite of the sensuous fog that threatened to engulf it. You first met him two days ago.

Two days.

She said on a half-sob, 'No, Clay.'

Lips skimming the responsive hollow below her ear, he muttered, 'I didn't understand what incendiary meant until I kissed you. How the hell do you do it?'

Natalia pulled back from the perilous sanctuary of his arms; for a moment they tightened around her, and then he let her go, shocking her into bereavement. Longing for contact, her body drooped. She flung back her head, stiffened her legs, made her hands stay peaceably at her sides, her fingers stop yearning for his heat and power.

All she could call on was the formality inherited from her mother. 'Thank you for bringing me home,' she croaked, inwardly wincing at the ridiculous words.

Clay smiled, a slow, dangerous smile that didn't hide a purely masculine aggression. His predatory eyes promised no surrender. 'Thank you for expanding my experience,' he drawled. 'I've never been so affected by a kiss before—I'm glad it had the same impact on you.'

Only dogged stubbornness got the key in the lock. Desperately, Natalia pushed the door open and stepped inside.

Sudden incredulity replaced the heat in the leonine depths of Clay's eyes before they turned curiously opaque. Clumsily Natalia went to shut the door against him, but he followed her, walking past her into the kitchen and the room that stretched out from it—a room bare of all furniture except an ancient armchair and a battered kitchen table, with one chair that had cost her a few dollars in the local secondhand shop.

The fire and passion of the past few minutes retreated, overtaken by stiff pride. With angry, lowered lashes she watched as he stood in the bleak room and stared around, his studied survey eventually lighting on the gallery of meticulously detailed pencil sketches pinned to one wall—mostly flowers and leaves from the bush, but some still lifes.

'Who did those?' he asked harshly.

'I did.' And, because it didn't matter any more, she added, 'At high school.'

He didn't look at her. 'They're very good.'

Holding her shoulders so erect she could feel the tension of abused muscles right down her spine, she asked with a frigid half-smile, 'What do you know about art?'

He met and matched her stare. 'Enough to know that a person with a talent like this should be using it, not growing capsicums.' He paused, his brows meeting above his nose. As if the question had been goaded from him, he demanded, 'Why capsicums?'

'My major creditors,' she said with exquisite courtesy, 'sat down with me when my father died and worked out a budget. The capsicums and the cattle were their idea, and I make an excellent income from them.'

He cast an aggressive glance around the room. 'And every cent you can save goes to pay off the loan?'

'Naturally.' Sometimes she thought she'd never get there, but each month the bank statement showed her she was slowly winning.

'What are you going to do when you've finally paid it off?'

'I'm going to revel in my freedom,' she returned fiercely, gripped by a complex mixture of grief and pain and anger. 'I'm going to wallow in it, and I'm never going to be tied down to anything again.'

His eyes narrowed, his features suddenly grim and calculating. 'Or any person?'

'Or any person,' she agreed, banking her swift, angry passion. 'I've had enough of responsibility; I'll do whatever I want, go wherever I please.'

He gave a short, hard laugh. 'I don't blame you for wanting freedom,' he said. 'In your place I would too. Let me have that quote to fix your tunnel-house as soon as it comes in.'

As she watched him go she touched an involuntary finger to her lips, touched Clay's mouth through it, and shivered with the hunger that ate away at her self-possession, her pride and her strength, the only things she'd managed to retain from the wreckage of her dreams. The transient pleasures of an affair promised meagre satisfaction, yet she didn't know what she wanted from Clay—certainly not to fall in love with him!

Because when Clay looked at her, all he saw was a woman to take to bed.

By the evening of the next day the effects of waking every two hours to check the irrigation system were making themselves plain, so after dinner Natalia went straight to bed. That night she had to force herself out each time her alarm clanged in her ear, and the last time she found herself staring at the dials and gauges with no idea of what she was looking for.

A sullen, smouldering sky at daylight promised rain, so once she'd packed and taken the capsicums to the transport depot she decided to dig over a piece in the vegetable garden. The hens went with her, scratching happily amongst the cabbages and broad beans in the sun, their friendly noises a pleasant and comforting accompaniment.

Half an hour later, when their amiable clucking changed in tone, she looked up to see a tall figure walking around the side of the house.

Driving the spade into the ground, she straightened up and watched Clay approach, her senses waking into clamorous, imperative life. He gave her a hard-eyed look that took in the hens, scattering now, and the freshly dug patch of ground.

'How much have you got left to do?' he asked.

'Good morning, Clay,' she said sedately. 'It's a lovely day, isn't it?'

His beautiful mouth curved—so classically perfect in shape that she tended not to realise its strength.

'I'm not a great one for preliminaries,' he said, pulling the spade out of the ground. 'Where do you want to dig to?'

For a crazy moment she thought of trying to reclaim the spade. Only for a moment, however, before common sense kicked in, controlling her irritation. He had good muscles; why not let him use them?

'Wise woman,' he said ironically, divining her thoughts with insulting accuracy. 'Not that I'd mind wrestling with you, but I can think of better places to do it.'

'Some people,' she snapped, removing herself to a patch of seedling lettuces that sorely needed weeding, 'might consider that to be sexual harassment.'

With smooth, economical movements he began to dig. 'Really?' he asked in a bland voice that set her teeth on edge. 'I don't intend to force you to do anything you don't want to, Natalia. I wouldn't enjoy an unwilling woman beneath me in bed.'

Colour scorched her skin. Keeping her head down, she crouched beside the lettuces and set to picking out weeds.

'And don't tell me you're too busy,' he said.

In a dignified silence Natalia ignored him. After a few minutes the hens resumed their chatty commentary, and the sun heated up, giving the lie to the red sky at dawn.

Studiously avoiding the sight of Clay digging, Natalia

found herself thinking that it was more than pleasant to work with someone in the cool, sweet air, to hear the clean sound as the spade sliced into the earth, the muted thud as the earth was transferred to its new position.

When the rhythmic swing of the spade stopped she looked up, her mouth drying as she saw him take off his shirt and toss it over a convenient post. Her hand trembled; jerking her gaze away, she blinked and stared at the green fuzz of weeds, only relaxing when the quiet sounds of his digging began again.

Unfortunately for any peace of mind, that momentary image was now imprinted on the insides of her eyelids—heavily muscled arms, broad shoulders and a chest filigreed by fine dark hair that scrolled across the golden skin then arrowed down to the belt of his jeans. Clay didn't have the carefully sculpted torso of a gym addict; his were muscles earned by physical labour.

Doing what? Tycoons usually looked soft and pudgy, but he certainly knew his way around a spade.

Natalia's stomach clamped into a knot. He'd been overwhelming in evening clothes, but like this he epitomised the kind of elemental male that inhabited the wilder reaches of female fantasy.

And let's not forget, she reminded herself, that he's also arrogant, rich, and determined to get me into bed. Danger in jeans.

'Right, that's it,' he said.

She waited until she was sure he'd put his shirt on again before looking up and awkwardly scrambling to her feet. 'Thank you,' she said in a stilted voice.

'I enjoyed doing it,' he said casually. 'We'll go and put that wheel on now, and before you say anything, I spoke to the woman who drives the post van and she told me she'd dropped it off this morning.'

'I can put it on myself, you know,' she said, reining in her temper with such determination that each word sounded dull and mechanical.

'I'm sure you can do anything you want to.' His smile taunted her. 'Except, perhaps, remove the shadows from under your eyes. Haven't you been getting enough sleep?'

'Plenty,' she said. 'Look, Clay, you're being a good neighbour—'

His laughter stopped her—low and sexy, the tinge of mockery in it had her clutching for control.

Biting the words between her teeth, she commanded, 'Don't you laugh at me!'

Lazy golden eyes scanned her face with indolent, chilling amusement. 'It would probably do you the world of good to laugh at yourself a bit more,' he said quite gently. 'You might be used to twisting every man who comes near you around your little finger, but I don't twist easily.'

'No, you're entirely too accustomed to getting your own way!' she flashed back, oddly exhilarated in spite of her anger.

He grinned. 'Indeed I am. We're two of kind, you and I. Now, either you come with me and we put this wheel on together, or I go down and put it on by myself.'

'You can go down and put it on yourself,' she said, backing off. The pleasure of being linked with him was too suspicious to be tolerated.

'Scared, Natalia?'

She snorted. 'Not in the least. I simply have more important things to do than stand by and be impressed when you take your shirt off again...' Appalled, she stopped, because that wasn't what she'd intended to say. Embarrassment clogged her throat.

'Did you like what you saw?' he asked, brows raised. 'All right, I'll go down and put the wheel on. But if I want to take my shirt off, sweetheart, I'll do that whether you're watching me from beneath your lashes or not.' He paused, then added, 'I don't care what people think about me.'

Something in his voice—some hidden, flat note—lifted her head sharply. The tiny hairs across the back of her neck stood up straight, warning her of danger. She'd hit a nerve there.

'Yes, you're intrigued,' he said in a dark drawl. 'Those green eyes are glinting, and your smile has a gleam of satisfaction in it. I might want you, Natalia, but I'm not going to let you tie a knot around my heart like you have with young Phil up there. When we make love it's going to be an honest transaction.'

Transaction? With stinging clarity she recalled Dean Jamieson's offer to settle her debt if she'd agree to ignore his wife and be his mistress. In a deadly voice, she asked, 'And is all this neighbourly assistance an attempt to prepay your way?'

An ugly light flared in his eyes, to be doused almost as soon as it appeared. 'I told you, I've never paid for sex in my life, Natalia.'

'How lucky you are,' she said sweetly. 'It must help that you're reasonably good-looking, with nice broad shoulders and a very handsome car. And you're rich.'

She'd expected him to lose his temper at the insult, but although his jaw tightened there was sudden, stunned understanding in the topaz eyes. 'How many men have tried to bribe their way into your bed?' he asked calmly. 'Phil?'

'No!'

'Then who?'

'Nobody,' she lied, afraid of his perceptiveness.

He came across to her, standing close enough so that she could smell the fresh, salty scent of sweat—sweat he had expended on her behalf. 'Natalia,' he said forcefully, his eyes clear and intent and unyielding, 'I don't see you as someone to be bought. Perhaps the word "transaction" was a mistake; I used it because I want what happens between us to be honest, without lies and evasions. Yes, I want to make love to you, but I also like and respect you. I admire your sense of responsibility, and the fact that you sold everything you could to pay off as much of your father's debt as you could.'

'What else could I do?' she asked stiffly, wondering why 'like' and 'respect' were not the words she wanted to hear him use.

His smile was ironic. 'You? Nothing. That's the difference between you and your father. He spent his life dreaming, following every wild-goose chase, every hare-brained scheme for making money from the land.'

Natalia said in a low, furious voice, 'He was a good man.'

'I'm sure he was.' Clay didn't try to hide his contempt. 'A selfish, charming good man. Liz told me you wanted to be a botanist, but because he needed your help you left school early and worked with him. He should have insisted you finish your education.'

'My mother was sick,' Natalia said stonily, swivelling away to pick up the spade.

But Clay got to it before she could and slung it over one shoulder. 'Didn't anyone—teachers, principal, friends—stick up for your right to a life of your own?'

Striding back to the shed where she kept her tools, she said in a harsh, unemotional voice, 'Oh, yes, but what else could I do? I knew my mother was dying.'

He looked down at her, and in that disciplined, determined glance she understood the difference between her father, a weak man for all his charm, and the man beside her. 'No child of mine,' Clay said calmly, 'will ever be robbed of her childhood or her education.'

Later—much later—Natalia would wonder if that was the moment she began the slippery, exultant slide into love. Until then she'd been fighting a fierce, elemental attraction; that level statement built the foundations of something much more stable, much more timeless than a heated desire.

Without pausing, he went on, 'How long will it take you to pay off the amount you owe?'

'How long's a piece of string?' she asked, using flippancy to cover her raw emotions.

'So you're still in hock to your father's dreams of Xanadu.'

'There's no alternative,' she said with crisp finality, wrenching on the toolshed door.

Of course it stuck, and of course Clay put the spade down and took over, hauling the wretched thing back with a powerful jerk as he said dispassionately, 'Sometimes filing for bankruptcy is the best thing to do.'

Natalia lifted her head. 'Not for me.' She hesitated, then went on, wanting him to understand, 'I'm managing, Clay— I don't go without food or clothes, and I am repaying the debt.'

'At what cost?' Beneath the cool, almost judicial tone rasped hidden emotions. He put the spade inside the shed and stood a moment, surveying the contents. 'You'll be marooned here for who knows how many years, working your guts out, missing out on everything other women of your age take for granted.'

She opened her lashes wide, smiling in a manner that should have alarmed him. 'But you're going to make my life much more exciting, aren't you?' she purred.

He grinned, his eyes molten and bright, but said laconically, 'Believe it. Why isn't there a lock for this? Don't you have a problem with farm thefts here?' He pushed the door closed.

She stepped back. 'Thieves go for farm bikes, quads, that sort of thing. They're not interested in my tools.' Without waiting for him, she set off towards the house.

He caught her up in one stride. 'Nevertheless, you should get a lock.'

'Certainly, sir.' Her voice positively oozed agreement.

She heard him laugh quietly. 'Please.'

The simple request made her heart flip. Before she could stop herself she gave him a sideways glance; her insides lurched when she met eyes as golden and uncompromising as the sun.

'I've got a padlock or two spare,' he told her. 'I'll come down and put one on.'

'Do you travel with spare padlocks?' she asked with false

interest. 'What exciting times you must have! I'm not the local deserving poor, thank you, so you don't need to come flashing your bounty around me—' Shocked and dismayed, she clamped her mouth over the words that threatened to surge forth.

A shimmering tension in the air froze her. She met Clay's regard with a slight movement of her head, but no anger glimmered in the eyes that scrutinised her face. They were hard and compelling and speculative.

'I'm sorry,' she muttered. 'That was unforgivably rude. However, I don't need to be looked after. I'm sure you mean well, but I find it patronising when you ignore what I say.'

'I can see that.' He didn't appear angry, for which she was reluctantly grateful. 'If I promise not to trample over that prickly independence,' he said, 'will you allow me to help you put the wheel on? I know you're capable of doing it, but I promise you it will be easier for me.'

Natalia had to stop herself from blurting out that she wasn't normally a shrew. He was a man who'd take swift advantage of any hint of weakness; admitting that he affected her so strongly would definitely be a weakness.

'As you ask so nicely,' she said with a wry smile, 'of course you can. I don't like being ordered around, but I'm happy to accept help when it's offered.'

His brows rose. However, all he said was, 'I promise not to take my shirt off.'

The only way to deal with such open provocation was to ignore it, and fortunately they reached the house then so she was able to without making it obvious.

The shirt stayed on, and he was right, he made a much faster job of putting the wheel back on than she would have.

Smiling her thanks, she got in, turned the key and stared blankly when she heard a slow chug-chug-chug followed by the whirring of the starter motor.

'Turn it off—it's empty,' Clay commanded. 'Someone's probably siphoned off the petrol.'

CHAPTER FIVE

NATALIA struck her clenched fists once on the wheel and swore fluently and at some length.

When she finally ran down, Clay was laughing. 'You've got a wide command of some extremely esoteric oaths. I don't know what the Russian ones mean, but they sound magnificently malevolent. OK, hop out. I've got petrol at home.'

Still fuming, she obeyed. Phil, thank heavens, didn't appear while Clay collected petrol from the implement shed at Pukekahu.

'That should get you to the nearest garage,' Clay said after he'd emptied the jerrycan into the truck's tank.

'I haven't got my purse,' she said, 'but if you'd like to call in—'

'Don't push your luck,' he said evenly, 'or I'll send you a bill for time spent digging and putting on a wheel.' The golden eyes were no longer indolent; they burned with a steady fire that warned her to go no further.

With stiff politeness she returned, 'Then thank you for the petrol.' And couldn't resist the temptation to add, 'Although a bill for services rendered would be unenforceable without some sort of contract, surely? Or at least a written quote?'

He looked at her for a taut moment, until that sardonic, lopsided grin banished the tension. 'Get away home, Natalia; you can relax now because I'm going away for a week or so.'

Natalia missed him, the needling ache in her heart only soothed five days later when Liz came to Xanadu for a long afternoon the day before she left for England.

From her Natalia learned that Clay's dinner party had been a huge success.

'Everyone who's anyone in Bowden was there. Did you know that Clay's a millionaire?' Liz asked as they walked up to Xanadu's highest point of land.

'I'm not surprised.' Natalia looked over the yearling steers she'd reared the previous spring. 'But I bet he didn't say so.'

Liz laughed. 'Of course he didn't! Dad read an article about him in one of those business magazines. Clay used a legacy to buy shares when he was still at high school, and made a real killing—as well as being astute enough to get out of the stock market before the '87 crash.'

'Did Clay tell the journalist this?' Natalia simply couldn't imagine him revealing his life to a business magazine.

'No. The journo said he'd had to dig really hard—apparently Clay's a bit of a mystery man. Anyway, after he left school he decided there was a future in horticulture. Pukekahu is his first foray into farming, but he's got interests in vineyards and olive groves, and a truffle-growing operation in the South Island that's earning enormous amounts of overseas exchange.'

Greedy though she was for knowledge about him, Natalia said offhandedly, 'Truffles? Those French fungi that pigs dig up from tree roots? I didn't know we had them in New Zealand.'

Liz grinned. 'Perhaps we didn't until Clay arrived on the scene. Apparently they cost a million dollars a gram.'

'I don't think so!'

'Well, they're incredibly expensive.'

'He's an absentee landlord,' Natalia said bluntly.

'Rubbish. He's an investor. Someone—I think it was Mrs Russell, so I don't know that I'd take much notice of it, because she often gets things wrong—anyway, she said she thought Clay had some sort of family connection to the Freemans who owned Pukekahu before Dean Jamieson.'

'Clay has? He's never said.' Would he have mentioned it? Probably not. 'Old Mr Freeman's daughter was Dean's stepmother. She died quite young.'

'So that's how he came to own it.' Liz panted up a small hill, skirting thriving bushes as she went. At the top she said, 'And that's probably the connection that Mrs Russell was thinking of. Aren't you supposed to kill all this gorse?'

'I grubbed it in the spring, but it's been a great year for it and I can't afford to spray just now,' Natalia told her. 'You were the one who wanted to climb up here and look at the sea.'

'It's my favourite spot.' Determinedly Liz homed back to the subject of Clay Beauchamp. 'Someone else said Clay's got into forestry in a big way.'

Natalia shrugged. 'So he's far-sighted. I wonder what he plans for Pukekahu.'

'Somebody asked him, but he didn't say. He knows how to keep his mouth shut without offending people.' Liz drew in a deep, rapturous breath. 'Oh, this is glorious! Why didn't you go to his party, Nat? I couldn't believe it when I realised you weren't coming.'

'I didn't want to.'

Although Natalia's voice was light and steady she didn't fool her oldest friend, who persisted, 'Why?'

'My mother said you should never accept hospitality you couldn't return.'

Wriggling through the slack wires of an elderly fence, Liz said, 'You could return it.'

'How?' Natalia asked as she climbed after Liz.

'You could ask him to a picnic,' Liz said sternly.

'In winter?'

'Well, wait until the summer! For heaven's sake, Nat, you know he's interested in you, yet you're deliberately cutting yourself off.'

'Liz, leave it, OK? As soon as I've paid off Dad's debts

I'll go out with any man who asks me. Well, within reason! I just haven't got time at the moment. Or the energy.'

'You're afraid of him,' Liz accused. 'Well, not really him, I suppose—you're scared that you'll let him get to you like blasted Dean Jamieson did, and that he'll let you down as badly.'

Natalia bristled, then subsided, admitting, 'I suppose I am. I don't have much faith in my judgement when it comes to men—first Dean, and then Phil. Sometimes I wonder if I'm just as hopeless as my father, only in relationships instead of business.'

'Nonsense.' Liz frowned. 'I feel sorry for Phil, but he simply wasn't right for you.'

'I should have remembered that my mother used to say men and women can't be friends.'

'Your mother was a very sophisticated lady, but I think she was wrong. Phil's got no right to carry on as though you've broken his heart—especially when he's taking another woman out!' Liz grasped a head of rushes to pull herself up a bank. 'As for Dean—well, it would have been very easy to lose your head over him. He's gorgeous—all tall and blond and laughing, with those sexy dark eyes— but he works too hard at being charming, you know?'

'I know,' Natalia agreed grimly.

'Yes. Clay doesn't have to work at it. He's got that terrific magnetism, and he's clever and sort of dynamically masterful, but he has a basic integrity you can't miss. And did you notice—men like and admire and respect him too? They didn't like Dean.'

'I must have been a total idiot to let him fool me.'

'Only for a little while,' Liz said quickly. 'You soon saw through him.'

Natalia said with dry self-derision, 'I was crazy for him, but when I found out about his wife it just evaporated— pouff! Like mist in the sun. I'm a lot more sensible now.' And she hoped it was true.

'It's not *sensible* to shut yourself away in case someone

hurts you again! Nat, I worry about you—you don't smile nearly as much as you used to, and that control is getting a bit scary.'

'I'm fine.' She smiled deliberately. 'I promise to smile at least ten times a day, and to lose my temper occasionally. You'd have been proud of me when I realised some louse had siphoned the petrol from the truck. I threw a proper tantrum, dredging up some of my grandfather's meatiest Russian curses.'

And Clay had laughed, a deep, sexy laugh that lit up his eyes and sent a kind of hot chill through every nerve in her body.

'I'll bet it did you the world of good.' Liz knew when to push, when to stay silent. 'Keep in touch,' she said. 'One letter a week.'

'You won't have time to write one letter a week.'

'Don't be an idiot, of course I will. And if I don't get a letter every week I'll set my mother on to you.'

She would too, and Mrs Kaiwhare had a ferocious maternal streak that would bring her storming up to Xanadu to see what the problem was. 'One letter a week,' Natalia promised. She stopped and turned. 'There, look at that.'

Around them whispered a cool breeze, sweet and tangy. The hills fell away in graceful folds to the sea, a brilliant silver-blue under the radiant sky. On the horizon islands lay like forgotten dreams.

'Nat, I don't want to go,' Liz said shakily.

'You'll have a ball. Think of blissfully diving into archives, and those wonderful old houses, and think of all the museums and libraries and theatres and nightclubs and the shops, Liz—think of all the shops!'

'At the moment it doesn't seem much recompense for all this,' Liz admitted. 'What are you looking at?'

Natalia frowned at a tractor working on Pukekahu. 'Phil must be stockpiling the materials for the new fence around the boundary.' She turned away, smiling at her friend. 'Don't forget us.'

'As if I could!'

Half an hour later, beside Liz's car, they hugged. 'I know I'm going to enjoy it when I get there,' Liz said, wet-eyed. 'You take care of yourself, all right? And for heaven's sake, if Clay Beauchamp asks you out, say yes and wear that green dress.'

'And you enjoy Oxford. Find yourself a Regency buck.'

Liz grinned. 'I'll have fun trying.'

Natalia waved the car off, closing her eyes so that she didn't see it disappear out of sight—one of her mother's superstitions. Then she checked the hydroponic system again.

She glanced at her watch. Yes, she had enough time to satisfy her curiosity about the heap of materials on the boundary fence.

It was surprising that Clay hadn't got in a team of contract fencers, but no doubt he had a reason for setting Phil to do it. Well, Natalia thought sarcastically as she crawled under her electric fence, of course there'd be several excellent reasons, apart from the fact that he didn't want her to do it! Clay Beauchamp wasn't a man who worked by instinct or emotion. The cool depths of those amber-gold eyes suggested that he based all his decisions on coldly rational motives—and the bottom line.

Except that he'd been kind in his acerbic way to her. But then, if you intended to make a woman your mistress, kindness was a good thing to cultivate! And he hadn't been coldly rational—or thinking of the bottom line—when he'd kissed her.

Squelching an excitement that threatened to get out of control, Natalia stopped to admire the small, pure white flowers of a manuka, then made her way out of the scrub on to the swamp.

The equipment for the boundary fence was impressive—large piles of wooden battens, concrete strainer posts and coils of wire all neatly stacked. A lot of money wrapped up in materials. Pukekahu would bloom with all this attention.

'Natalia!'

Phil, she realised, with a swift dread founded on her smarting conscience. Beaming, he walked jauntily around the heap of battens. Too late she saw a flash of red from the tractor behind the fencing materials. She hesitated, but Phil waved, and with a hidden reluctance she picked her way across the swamp, jumping from one clump of tussocks to another until she reached the stream that drained it.

There she stopped, using the metre-wide creek as a psychological barrier. 'Hello, Phil,' she said, striving to sound friendly but non-committal.

His eyes devoured her. 'Hi, Natalia.' He struggled with himself, but his question was swift and jealous. 'Have a good time at the masquerade ball?'

'Yes, it was great fun.' Before he had a chance to reply she tacked on, 'How's Rachel?' Rachel was the pleasant woman who'd been in love with him for years.

'She's all right.' He jumped the creek and came towards her, his good-looking face starkly outlined. 'Natalia,' he began. 'Please, Natalia, couldn't we at least talk—?'

She held out her hands in the time-honoured gesture of repudiation. 'I'm sorry,' she broke in, hating to hurt him all over again, yet angry with him for not accepting that their very mild relationship was over—had died stillborn. And she was tired of feeling guilty! 'Phil, we've already talked and I don't—'

'Please,' he said, his voice cracked and desperate. He reached for her and snatched her close, trying to kiss her with a raw, frenzied hunger that appalled her. 'Please, darling,' he whispered, 'please don't turn me away—'

When Clay had touched her she had forgotten every maxim of the self-defence classes she'd attended; not so now. She could hurt Phil quite severely, but although she could never love him he was a nice man.

'No,' she said firmly, pushing at him. 'Phil, stop this! *Stop it!*'

He gabbled wretchedly, 'I can't; God knows, I've tried,

but I can't. I know you've never loved me, but you've gutted me, Natalia. I can't stop loving you.'

'You could if you tried—you just haven't given it long enough.' The inflexible male voice froze them both.

Natalia flinched as Phil's arms fell away from her and a dark, painful colour patched his cheekbones. Instinctively protective, she swivelled to face Clay, her chin angling upwards.

He'd stopped a few metres away, his expression an intimidating mix of authority and lack of tolerance as his voice cut through the taut silence like a whiplash. 'Until then, don't do your courting on my time—especially as it's so clearly not welcome. You've got another load of stuff to deliver.'

Phil's jaw tightened. Without looking at Natalia he muttered, 'All right,' and walked doggedly away.

Natalia waited with the wary aggression of a duellist until the tractor started up and roared up the hill.

Before she could speak Clay said in a lethal voice, 'I told you not to torment him.'

'I didn't know he was here.' Even to her it sounded lame. Almost vibrating with antagonism, she added, 'And I don't take orders from you.'

'While he's working for me you'll stay out of his way unless you want to see him sacked.'

Dry-mouthed, she stared at the relentless framework of his face in the winter sunlight. She said, 'He doesn't deserve that. And you needn't worry—I don't want to encourage him,' finishing with a snap, 'either on your time or his.'

'So why did you come down here?' Clay asked with unsparing insistence.

The incident with Phil must have upset her more than she'd realised because she said, 'I was just curious.'

'And now you've satisfied it, you can forget about the fence,' he said softly, his golden eyes half-closed as they roamed her face. They came to rest on her mouth, and narrowed into sudden, dangerous slits.

She jerked back as he took two strides towards her. 'He hurt you,' he said harshly, touching her upper lip with a long forefinger.

Natalia said indistinctly, 'No.'

Clay stroked across the generous curve. Her eyes stayed fixed on his shirt button, but that light caress melted every bone in her body.

'Your lip is swollen.'

Startled by the ferocious undertone to his statement, she looked up into eyes cold as crystallised fire. 'He didn't hurt me,' she protested. 'Phil wouldn't hurt anyone.'

'You're remarkably innocent,' Clay said grimly. 'It looked as though he was forcing you to stand still while he kissed you. In my book, that's violence.' His finger traced the edge of her lips, lightly, almost possessively, as though staking a claim. 'If you want that pretty face to remain unmarked you'd better learn to recognise men who are capable of it.'

His touch seared through her, scrambling her mind, confusing her. Stepping back, she repeated, 'Phil would never hurt me—or anyone else.'

'He'd better not,' Clay said harshly. 'Keep away from him. I don't want him mooning around because he wants you and can't get you. To someone in his state, even a casual meeting and a flash of that singularly provocative smile is encouragement.'

Unfortunately he was right. Natalia said stiffly, 'Thank you for the advice. I'll leave you now.'

Some other, more suspect emotion lit the golden embers in his eyes to a muted life. 'Do you have to?'

Quite deliberately he moved closer, filling her with a feverish panic.

Natalia's heart began to pick up speed. Because she wasn't going to let him see that she was intimidated, she nodded and said casually, 'See you later,' as she turned away and began to thread her way across the spongy ground.

He caught up to her with a couple of long silent strides,

saying conversationally, 'You smell of flowers.' And as her eyes widened, he added, 'Wild flowers.'

She recognised the mockery in his gaze and in the curve of his hard mouth, and squared her shoulders. 'Ragwort,' she said sweetly, taking the opportunity to step over a puddle and away from him. 'Or perhaps it's gorse.'

'Thistles?' he suggested, the gleaming topaz gaze darkening as it dropped for another fraught second to her mouth.

Natalia turned her head and gave him a smile that stopped just short of baring her teeth. 'No thistles,' she said, grabbing at the strap-like leaves of a flax plant to haul herself over a patch of ground turned to oozy mud by the hooves of cattle. 'I grubbed them out last spring.'

His brows twitched together, but he said merely, 'You don't need to point out how tough you are, Natalia. I know.'

'I work the farm, so of course I'm strong.' It irritated her that he managed the bog as easily and lithely as he'd waltzed.

'Graceful too.'

Struggling to retain her poise, she said, 'How kind of you.'

'But you don't believe it?' A taunt underlaid the question.

She said formally, 'I enjoy a compliment as well as anyone. Even if I don't really deserve it.'

Mockery showed for a moment in the angular face. 'When people refute a compliment it's often because they want to be convinced of it.'

'That's a cynical thing to say,' she retorted, feeling colour burn through her skin. Anger, she decided staunchly, not embarrassment.

As she angled her chin he said unexpectedly, 'Yes, it was.' Those tawny-gold eyes were now cool and dispassionate, the deep voice withdrawn, hawkish features under masterful control.

Chilled, Natalia stopped by the scrub that clothed the side of the gully. Crisp and bracing, the scent of damp manuka enclosed them. 'I'll see you around, then. Goodbye.'

His mouth curved in a tilted, unpleasant smile. He'd stopped as well and was looking at her, his eyes alert and far too perceptive. 'I'll walk you home. There might be other lovelorn swains around.'

'Not a one, I promise. I don't need to be escorted,' she said politely. 'I can look after myself.'

'I saw how capable you are. He was mauling you and all you were doing was saying *stop*. You should have hit him in the solar plexus.'

The icy distaste in his voice made her blink. 'I'm not frightened of Phil,' she said, exasperated because he wouldn't listen.

'Nevertheless, stay away from him.' Clay's voice was cold and specific. Before she could respond he asked, 'Have you got your wasp pills with you?'

She clapped a hand on the back pocket of her jeans. 'Yes,' she said in a clipped voice.

He smiled and stepped back. 'Then off you go,' he said blandly.

For a furious moment she stared at him, until the amusement in his eyes burned through her stupid disappointment.

'Goodbye,' she said frigidly and strode into the moist dimness of the scrub, fuming all the way to the house.

Once inside she poured herself a glass of water and went out on to the verandah to drink it, looking out over her paddocks. Cattle grazed with afternoon enthusiasm, the westering sun picking out their hides so that they glowed. On her way in she'd let out the hens; they were now busily scratching up their quota of seeds and insects in the paddock. Only the tunnel-houses were ugly in their hi-tech plastic, like huge, stumpy white caterpillars, but between the cattle and the capsicums she was keeping her head above water.

As she was doing with Clay. Her mouth relaxed into a mirthless smile. Treading water wasn't as glamorous or inspiring as striking out for the shore, but it kept you out of danger.

Falling in love left you too vulnerable, too open to pain. Poor Phil had found that out. In spite of the electricity that sang through her whenever she saw Clay, she wasn't going to give him any chance to break her heart.

She drained the glass of water and went back inside, frowning at the mail she'd dumped that morning. The bank envelope sent a shiver through her, but although tempted to ignore it she firmed her lips and slit the envelope, then checked the statement inside.

'What on earth...?' she said slowly, because the balance on the page was far more than it should be. Common sense told her it was a mistake, but hope glimmered while she read down the credits. Perhaps she was the one who'd made the mistake and she was much better off than she—

A name leapt out at her. Clay had paid in an outrageous sum of money to her credit.

The sheet of paper jerked as her fingers tightened on it. It took all her control to relax them, to put the paper down on the bench and draw in a ragged breath.

Never take on anyone when you're angry, her father used to say. Wait until it's died down.

With an odd sort of detachment she realised she was shaking. The very strength of her reaction frightened her. She'd never felt like this before, not even when Dean had admitted that he was married, then suggested it made no difference.

'Calm down,' she muttered as if it was a mantra. 'Calm down, calm down, calm down...'

But she had to go out and dig in her garden until the sun had gone before she'd exhausted her anger. Even then, while she showered and deliberately chose clean jeans and a sweatshirt that came close to being an antique, rage smouldered away inside her.

Tamping it down, she rang Pukekahu, only to get Phil in the manager's cottage.

It hurt to hear the eagerness in his voice. 'I'm sorry,' she said tiredly. 'Phil, I'd forgotten there was no phone in the homestead—I didn't mean to interrupt you.'

She sensed that he was pulling himself together. 'Did you want Clay? He has a mobile number—but I don't know whether I should give it to you.'

'Don't bother,' she said.

'I suppose I should have expected it,' he said curtly. 'He's a much better catch than I am. I'll ring him and tell him you want to contact him.'

Natalia bit back the angry words—she had no need to justify herself to Phil. Besides, he might finally understand she had nothing but friendship to offer him if he believed she was chasing Clay. 'I'm sorry,' she repeated briskly, and hung up.

Life would have been much simpler if she could have fallen in love with Phil. He was a kind, decent man.

She'd only taken a couple of steps away from the phone when it rang.

'You wanted to contact me?' Clay's deep voice was abrupt. 'Have you got a pen? Copy down this number.'

'I won't need it again,' she said, each word curt and distinct.

There was a brief pause. 'So you got your bank statement today. All right, I'm on my way.'

'I don't—' The phone went dead.

Natalia stood with her fists clenched at her sides, fighting her desire to run and change into something more feminine, more attractive than the elderly sweatshirt and faded jeans. She'd been too angry to do anything about dinner or lighting the fire, and now a chill was creeping up from the floor and she had a hollow instead of a stomach.

How dared Clay think she could be bought? She wanted to shout at him and rage against whatever fate had made her so attracted to him. But not in her bare, cold house with its pathetic sticks of cheap furniture and her even more pathetic reminders of lost dreams pinned on the wall.

She took several quick strides across, intending to rip the sketches down, then stopped.

No, she wasn't ready to surrender them yet. Not yet...

Filling the kettle with water, she switched it on and waited tensely for the sound of his big car. Just as the kettle boiled it came quietly out of the night; she got down two mugs and a tea caddy and made a pot of tea.

Nerves jumping, she waited for the knock. When it finally came, she walked out and opened it, standing back to let Clay in.

He was suffocatingly large in the almost empty room that had once been a pleasant, comfortable sitting room; it didn't seem fair, she thought fleetingly, that he should have so much sheer male presence!

'Sit down,' she said stonily, waving at the armchair.

'No, thank you.' He sounded contemptuous. 'What's your problem?'

'You know what it is. Why did you put seven hundred dollars into my account?'

'Don't be obtuse. My steer broke through your electric fence and trashed at least some of your tunnel-house. I pay my debts.'

The colour drained from her face. His eyes darkened and he swore beneath his breath. 'Damn it, Natalia, I didn't mean that you don't!'

'Then what did you mean?'

'As you pointed out, I owed you for the damage and for the loss of quite a few plants.'

'Seven hundred dollars' worth?'

He didn't move, but she sensed a discomfort in him, a moment of hesitation. Whipping up her anger, she said, 'I may be poor, but I don't sponge off my neighbours.'

'Natalia.' He said her name as though it was something precious to him. 'You're shivering,' he said curtly. 'It's bloody cold in here—don't tell me you have no heating!'

It wasn't the cold making her shiver; tormented by a wild

hunger made more potent by her emotion, she stood with green eyes glittering, her mouth a straight, tight line.

'Use some of the money to get a heater,' he snarled.

'Are you trying to buy me?'

'Why would I be so stupid? You want me every bit as much as I want you!' Clay's iron restraint was splintering, its cracks revealing a white-hot anger to match hers. 'You know what you're doing, don't you? You're using every excuse you can to push me away.'

He reached her in one stride and lifted her hands, his own making steel bracelets around her wrists. When Natalia shuddered he dropped them and picked her up as easily as if she'd been half her size. 'I won't let you starve yourself and go cold out of misplaced pride,' he said savagely, eyes hard and uncompromising, his mouth a straight line. 'If it means so much to you, give me back the extra money after you've taken out the amount that covers the damage my steer did. And make sure you count the previous times it got into your tunnel-house.'

His arms tightened around her, holding her against his charged body. He was so hot, she thought feverishly, and she leaned into that heat, warming herself at it like a child bewitched by the dangerous beauty of a bonfire. It was all she could do to say, 'I'm not starving myself.'

'You haven't had anything to eat, have you? There are no cooking smells.'

'I've been digging.'

'Come out to dinner with me.' His voice was deep, almost husky, all anger gone.

A moment ago she'd been so furious she could barely speak. Now it had seeped away, leaving her raw and vulnerable. All she wanted to do was lie there in his strong arms and abandon herself to the language of her senses, to glory in the power and heat of his big body, to watch the movement of his mouth as he spoke, to let the scent that was a mixture of soap and subliminal male pheromones work their magic on her.

'Natalia?' He set her on her feet, lifting her chin so that he could see into her dazed eyes.

Almost lost to prudence, she welcomed the excuse. 'I can't—I have to be here at nine o'clock.'

'Why?'

She was in deep trouble, because the swift question didn't do any more than burnish her caution. 'I need to check the peppers.'

'Then have dinner with me at Pukekahu,' he said urgently. 'I can't leave you like this.'

For a shocked moment she was tempted. But she pulled away from the haven of his arms, saying stupidly, 'I'd rather keep this businesslike—'

'How can you?' he asked, smiling the lopsided smile that twisted her heart. 'We saw each other and wanted each other—it happened in the first minute. Business has got nothing to do with it, and you know it.'

'Are you married?' she asked abruptly, watching him with suspicious eyes.

He laughed, but his eyes were level. 'No. No marriage, no engagement, no relationship.'

'Then I'll come out to dinner,' she said.

'If you need to be back by nine I can organise that. Do you like spicy food?'

'Very much.'

'Then we'll go to The Indies. It does Indonesian food very well.'

Who else had he taken there? Shaking her head, she looked down at her jeans. 'I haven't got—'

'Wear the clothes you had on when you came up to the homestead—the shirt that's the same colour as your eyes.' He glanced at his watch. 'While you're changing I'll book a table and tell them we need to be in and out in two hours.'

It wasn't until she'd got to her room and pulled off her jeans and sweatshirt that she worked out his tactics. Just take things for granted and dimwits like Natalia Gerner would meekly go along with him.

But a febrile anticipation built inside her, burning away the cautious prompting of common sense. What harm could going out to dinner with him do?

It could break her heart, that was what it could do, because she suspected she was heading down a long and lonely path—a path towards love for a man who hadn't said anything about love, a man who made no bones about wanting a mistress.

So what? she thought defiantly. You got over the last dented heart soon enough. Do it often enough and you'll get used to it.

And anyway, could love grow from this powerful, violent physical response? How would she know the difference? After all, she'd wanted Dean too—although not like this.

But even as she got into her clothes she knew there was no comparison between Dean Jamieson's facile charm—based on sexual promise and superficial courtesy and a fundamental disrespect for women—and Clay, as protective as he was dominant, who seemed to understand both her inconvenient sense of responsibility and her desire for freedom.

CHAPTER SIX

When she walked back into the sitting room and saw him waiting, her pulses gave a sudden, almost deafening thump. He'd been examining her sketches and he turned as she came in and watched her come towards him. A cotton shirt in a shade of copper lit his eyes to molten ore, and his mouth was curled in a smile that both beckoned and taunted.

'You look like something wild and woodstruck,' he said, scanning her with deliberate enjoyment. 'Beautiful and pagan and free.'

It threw her; he had no right to unseat her with a sly, practised compliment. Coolly she returned, 'You look splendid too. Did you get a table at The Indies?'

'Yes, and told them we were in a hurry. Why do you have to be back by nine?'

'I have to check the hydroponics system,' she said. She said it casually, as though this was an entirely normal thing for her to do.

She should have known better. 'No doubt because as well as trashing your plants and eating the capsicums, the steer damaged it,' he said curtly. When she hesitated, he went on without finesse, 'Make sure you take the cost of the replacement out of the money I deposited.'

'Yes, sir,' she said sweetly.

He grinned at her barely hidden challenge, then frowned. 'Will you be warm enough like that?'

'I believe the restaurant has excellent heating.' She wasn't going to tell him she had nothing suitable to wear over her pretty green shirt.

'You have a real talent for ink and watercolour,' he said, nodding at the wall of sketches. 'Do you do any now?'

89

Natalia shook her head abruptly, her face still and proud. If he showed any sort of pity at all he could eat dinner by himself.

He didn't, although his eyes narrowed. 'Liz said you once had plans to be a botanist.'

Mentally adding a caustic page to the letter to Liz that lay half finished in her bedroom, Natalia said, 'When I was at high school. And even then I think it was only because I wanted to draw plants.'

'And now?'

She shrugged. 'One day, when I have more time, I'll probably take it up again.'

Dark lashes hid his thoughts, but to her relief he said no more about the sketches; as they drove to the restaurant she realised with surprise that she was glad he'd seen them. Now he knew there was something she could do well.

On the outskirts of Bowden, The Indies was new, stylish and expensive; it attracted guests from the coast as well as people in the immediate district. Natalia had never been there before. It seemed to her that every eye was on them as they were shown to their table, one set a little aside, about halfway between a huge black grand piano and the flickering flames of the fire. In spite of her prickly mood she couldn't squelch a lowering, embarrassing pleasure that she was with Clay Beauchamp.

Keeping her eyes fixed on the menu, she determinedly discussed the food until the waitress took their order.

After choosing a bottle of white wine, Clay said without preamble, 'I thought the easiest way to deal with the situation was simply to deposit money in your account.' He gave her a sardonic look. 'I assumed you'd use only what was necessary, itemise the accounts to the last cent, and take great pleasure in flinging any change back in my face.'

Natalia stopped herself from wetting suddenly dry lips. Was she being foolishly antagonistic? 'I—thank you for trusting me with—with the money. It's just that you overwhelm me.' Her voice sounded creaky so she swallowed. 'I'm sorry if I seemed ungrateful.'

'Gratitude is not what I want from you,' he returned negligently, the thin straight scar on his face lit for a second by the leaping light of the fire. 'Your father's shame is not yours, Natalia. Plenty of people endure hard times—it's nothing to be embarrassed about.'

Stung pride burned up through her skin. 'Even you?' she asked, trying to sound casual.

His eyes were hooded. 'Yes.' The answer was crisp and inflexible. 'After I left school I put every cent I could scrape up into investments in the rural sector, and because I needed to know what I was doing, I spent a lot of time working on farms.'

Natalia could imagine him harnessing his will to his ambition, using every ounce of determination and patience and endurance to build his empire. 'It must have been hard going,' she said quietly.

To build as much as he had, so swiftly, needed more than sheer hard work; Clay's empire was based on flair and nerve and a nose for a bargain, as well as an almost intuitive understanding of trends and opportunities.

'I enjoyed it,' he said simply. 'I took courses at various polytechs for the financial side of things, and I wheeled and dealed and lived on a surge of adrenaline for years. Like you, I had things to prove.'

What things?

Before she could ask the unwise question forming on her tongue he went on, 'Tell me why your parents decided to move here when neither of them knew anything about earning a living off the land.'

She shrugged. 'As you said, my father had a dream,' she told him, not trying to hide the irony in her words. 'He believed that living in cities was bad for humanity; he hoped that technology would enable us all to live in small communities in the country. He was convinced that when we did crime would dwindle and the world would be a much better place. So he went looking for Xanadu.'

'Did your mother agree with him?'

'She came with him; I suppose she did.' Although she'd found life in Bowden boring, she'd loved her husband.

'What made him think he could earn a living off ten hectares?'

'You *can* earn a living off ten hectares.'

'If you've got the capital to set up a proper system,' Clay said mercilessly.

Got it in one. Her father had always been so certain that every new project would make their fortune, remaining filled with optimism even though each venture had failed to live up to his rosy expectations.

Natalia didn't say anything, but she didn't need to. Clay would read her unspoken words with unerring comprehension. In a way it was a relief when he leaned back into the dining chair, one tanned hand resting with casual strength on the white tablecloth, and said, 'So you grow capsicums and fatten cattle. Do you rear them from calves?'

'The next lot arrive in July.'

His dark, straight brows drew together. 'How many?'

'Ten.'

'That's a real tie,' he said thoughtfully, the tawny gaze scrutinising her face until she felt stripped, so exposed she couldn't hide a vagrant thought.

The waitress came with bowls of hot, spicy soup. Thank heavens, Natalia thought edgily as the first fragrant mouthful slid down her throat.

'How long will it take you to pay off this mortgage?' Clay asked.

Natalia gave him an aloof look. 'I'm working on it,' she returned.

Watching her with half-closed eyes, he said, 'All to show the world that you aren't like your father. Looked at pragmatically it's a foolish burden to shoulder, but it was wholly admirable of you to take it on.'

A swift, hot shiver scudded down her spine. Crisply, and possibly unwisely, she said, 'I didn't want anyone to suffer for his faults—and his bad luck.'

'Anyone but you,' he said quietly.

Natalia's shoulders lifted in a shrug. She'd worn her grandmother's gold chain as a necklace beneath the green shirt, and the warm links moved against suddenly sensitised skin. 'Wouldn't you do the same thing if it had been your father?'

His hard, handsome face remote, he leaned back, slightly shifting the glass of wine so that the flames in the fireplace turned the liquid to golden-green elixir.

'I never knew my birth father,' he said.

'Then your adoptive father?'

The wine glass tilted. 'If he'd had debts, yes, I'd have paid them,' he said indifferently, 'even though we didn't like each other.'

Awkwardly Natalia said, 'I'm sorry.'

His abrupt nod acknowledged her sympathy. 'To get back to Xanadu, in a couple of years land prices will start to rise again.'

'Believe me, I'll sell you the place as soon as it's worth enough money to repay the debt.'

'And in the meantime you'll slog your heart out. And if you do sell, you'll end up with nothing.'

Trust him to home in on her other great worry. 'I don't work any harder than lots of people,' she said calmly. 'And most people start their life with no money.'

'Most people start when they leave school,' Clay said tersely, 'and acquire a few more qualifications than knowing how to grow capsicums and raise stock. Why couldn't your father have fallen in love with a more conventional block? Most of Xanadu is bush and gullies.'

'He wasn't looking for an investment property like Pukekahu.' What else could she say? The difference between her father and Clay was that Ryan Gerner had bought land because he'd fallen in love with it, whereas Clay chose his for cold, hard profit.

Yet, although Clay's iron integrity might break bones, he'd never allow an overwhelming optimism to cheat his friends of their savings.

'Pukekahu will be self-sufficient in less than two years, whereas anyone with an atom of common sense would have realised that without large injections of capital Xanadu would never be able to support itself—unless you found gold on it, and as far as I know that's not likely to happen.'

'Not in Northland,' she said, the words acrid on her tongue.

'So, what are your plans?'

'I'll manage,' she said with a proud lift of her chin, rejecting any pity.

His mouth tightened. 'How?'

'I'll manage,' Natalia repeated, converting her stubborn expression into a smile for the waitress who brought their main courses—fish cooked in coconut cream with lemongrass and chilli for Natalia, spicy beef for Clay.

When they were once again alone he said, 'In other words you haven't the faintest idea what you'll do. Your parents should be shot for leaving you in this situation.'

'They didn't do it deliberately,' she flashed back, her appetite suddenly deserting her.

'They didn't *die* deliberately,' he said with curt disregard for her feelings, 'but they sure as hell didn't make any provision for your future. They didn't even see that you had some sort of training so you could earn a decent living.'

'And yours did?' Natalia said shortly.

Clay's tawny gaze darkened into something compelling and stark. After a taut moment Natalia glanced down at the plate of food in front of her and picked up her knife and fork.

When he spoke his voice was detached, yet she heard a gritty note beneath each word, as though he had to force it out. 'God alone knows who my birth father was. My birth mother was killed in a car accident just after my sixth birth-day, leaving me without any relatives. I was made a state ward, and about a year later I was adopted. I adored my adoptive mother, but her husband didn't think much of me—he had a great belief in the purity of blood. He also had a son by a previous marriage, and I soon understood that no matter what I did I'd never measure up to him in our father's eyes.' He didn't sound scornful, but he didn't need to. It was obvious what he thought of his adoptive father.

Natalia's breath hissed through her lips. She couldn't bear the thought of him as a small, bewildered child. 'What did he want—Superboy?'

Broad shoulders lifted in a shrug. 'He probably could have coped with a pretty little girl. What he got was a savage. Olivia loved me and civilised me, and we managed to rub along reasonably well while she was alive. He wanted her, and if keeping her happy meant putting up with the kid she'd wanted them to adopt, well, he was prepared to do it. Things disintegrated fast after she died.'

'How old were you?' Natalia asked, her heart wrung.

'Sixteen.' Evenly he finished, 'I left home within six months.'

Natalia said fiercely, 'I'm so glad you've succeeded—it's by far the best revenge! He didn't deserve you for a son.'

He gave her an oblique glance. 'My birth mother wasn't a shining light of virtue, either. I don't remember much about her, but she used to hit me, and locked me up some-times when she went out. Olivia was my real mother, and it was her legacy that started me off.'

'I'm glad you had those years with her,' Natalia said even more fiercely. Her parents had both loved her. Perhaps Clay's lonely, harsh childhood explained the courage and initiative that had led to his success.

The waitress came over, smiled at them both, and asked how their meal was. Clay said, 'It's delicious, thank you.'

And when she'd left them, he observed, 'It's an unusual restaurant to find in a place like Bowden.'

Natalia bristled. 'Why?'

His lopsided smile teased her. 'Sophisticated cuisine in the middle of a farming district?'

'A lot of people in Bowden have travelled widely and lived overseas,' she said, relieved by the change of subject. 'It's quite a cosmopolitan place. I thought that was one of the reasons you bought Pukekahu.'

'I live in Auckland, remember?'

'What are your plans for the station?' she asked, wondering if he'd tell her to mind her own business.

He wasn't as blunt, although his smile was tinged with mockery. 'To turn it into a productive unit.'

'There's a lot to do,' she said. 'The previous owner ran it into the ground.'

'He squeezed it dry,' he said, and although he spoke without emphasis she felt a cold little clutch of nerves in her stomach.

'It will be great to watch it come back to life again.'

With cool adroitness Clay steered the conversation into local affairs, so that soon they were discussing a long-lived quarrel over the War Memorial Hall in Bowden. Delighted when she made him laugh by explaining the personalities and complicated district politics involved, Natalia forgot that she was far too attracted to this man—and that she knew even less about him than she had Dean Jamieson!

From the tangled, acrimonious affairs of the hall committee they drifted on to the state of the economy, and somehow ended up dissecting a novel that had set the literary establishment on its ears. So aware of him that her body was taut with expectation, Natalia sparred and talked and listened, and enjoyed herself enormously.

Until Phil walked in with Rachel and gave her a wounded stare. When Clay saw Natalia's smile die, he demanded, 'What's the matter?'

'Nothing,' she said, but of course he knew.

'What did you do to him?' he asked as Phil and Rachel were shown to a table on the other side of the room.

'I went out with him for two months,' she said shortly, 'that's all.'

'And because of that he acts as though you've ruined his life?'

Natalia didn't blame him for disbelieving her—Phil was certainly behaving oddly. She muttered, 'I don't want to talk about it.'

Relationships, affairs—she was no good at them. Eventually love died and desire fizzled out. Her experience with Dean should have been a salutary lesson; it wasn't Phil's fault that she hadn't learned it. He'd been hurt simply because she'd been foolish enough to want a pleasant companion, a male friend.

She didn't have the time or the emotional energy to cherish any sort of relationship.

Of course if she gave Clay what he so patently wanted she wouldn't have to find emotional energy; however you prettied it up, the sort of passion he spoke of was nothing more than nature's instinctive drive to reproduce.

The arrival of a large, brilliantly attired woman gave her a welcome break from her thoughts. Clay lifted an eyebrow as the woman sailed flamboyantly through the room.

'That's Soshanna,' Natalia murmured. 'She plays the piano—and is extremely good at it.'

He nodded, smiling as the woman caught his eye and gave him an intimate come-hither glance before seating herself with a flourish. His expression altered slightly; he looked experienced and sophisticated and a little cynical.

Yes, he knew how to handle himself. Probably no woman would ever break through that impervious self-containment to reach the heart beneath.

If he had a heart...

She'd read that children who weren't loved were damaged for life. Had Olivia's affection filled his empty heart and taught him how to love, or was Clay doomed to live his life by principles? Natalia's heart contracted; she was filled with a swift, aching desire to give him everything he'd missed in those wretched first six years of his life.

He surprised her by asking, 'How old were you when you moved up here?'

'Ten.' Her face softened. 'I adored it. I could run and run and run without having to worry about roads, and I used to stand at the top of the hill and pretend I was flying all the way out to the coast. And then I'd lie down and roll over and over to the bottom. My mother used to scold me for getting grass stains on my clothes, but my father understood.'

Suddenly embarrassed, she saw that his gaze was fixed on to her face, watchful, unfaltering, like that of the bird of prey she'd first thought he resembled. 'So you were uncaged,' he said, startling her with his perceptiveness. 'I didn't realise that freedom had always been so important to you.'

Soshanna had been playing quietly in the background, but at that moment the pianist slid into a moody piece, aching with grief and lost love, threaded with need. Natalia braced herself, then touched her heavy linen napkin to her lips, hiding behind it for a second.

'What is it?' Clay asked abruptly.

'Nothing.' She forced a cheerful note into her voice as she anchored the napkin in her lap with one hand.

Oh, Phil, she thought, wondering how she'd managed to arouse such emotions in a man she merely liked. When he'd told her this song spelled out everything he felt for her she'd severed their relationship—too late. Had he requested it, or was it just a coincidence?

She looked at Clay and felt a disturbing jolt of reaction. He was watching her with a cool, analytical regard, as though she was something to be studied.

This man, she thought ironically, would no more pour his heart out to a woman in a song than he'd fly over the moon. In an odd sort of way he was safe. There'd be no dramatic scenes with him—if they became lovers it would be on his terms, and when the end came he'd finish it quickly and cleanly.

And, she thought uneasily, she might be the one left with the broken heart.

Perhaps no more than she deserved.

The waitress appeared with a dessert menu. 'Just coffee, thank you,' Natalia said, watching with awe as Clay chose a pudding from the list.

He caught her expression and laughed, an intriguing sound, deep and sexy, with a note in it that promised a talent for sensuality. It was a laugh you could remember while you were going to sleep, a laugh to make you smile, dream irresponsible dreams.

'I have a sweet tooth,' he admitted.

And a large frame to keep going. Again she felt that disconcerting melting, the urgent, visceral twist of need that weakened her at the same time as it charged her with a hungry energy.

But she wasn't going to surrender to it. Why ask for trouble—however desirably it came wrapped? She had no space in her life for Clay. It was simply not sensible to break her heart over a man who wanted a relationship based only on sexual attraction.

She had to remind herself of this while she basked in his assured, intelligent charm. Exciting though it was to be treated with such unsettling attention, acutely aware though she was of him, an uneasy restlessness chased across her nerves. This disturbing intimacy, this adrenaline-charge of fascination, meant nothing, was going nowhere.

And she should be glad of it.

'That's a pensive look,' he observed calmly.

Perhaps something of her emotions showed in her expression, because he immediately said with lazy understanding, 'Pulling down the shutters, Natalia?'

'I don't know what you mean,' she evaded. Accustomed to men who had to be told in clear, distinct words what was wrong with the women in their lives, Clay's perceptiveness still startled her. His uncomfortably accurate conclusions indicated an extensive, threatening knowledge of women.

He smiled at her, his long-lashed gaze glinting with a tempting, dangerous magnetism. In a voice that was deep and smooth and sensual he said, 'I'm glad I overwhelm you, Natalia. You overwhelm me too. I look at you and I want to lose myself in you, take you so far and so high and so deep that you'll never remember what it was like before you met me.'

Her mouth dried. Everything that had happened to her until that moment had been a mere prelude, time to be endured before she had heard Clay say that he wanted her. For a second—a half-second—that terrifying, awe-inspiring feeling of rightness, of oneness, locked her in stasis, even drowning out the clamorous response of her body to his voice, his words, the heated possessiveness of his gaze as it rested on her mouth, and then flicked up and caught her with her heart in her eyes.

She shivered, and he asked harshly, 'Are the languishing stares in your direction worrying you? I can put a stop to them.'

Natalia realised who he meant just in time to stop herself from looking over her shoulder. 'I'm sure he's not languishing,' she said tautly. 'That makes Phil sound an idiot and he isn't; he's a nice man.' It wasn't his fault he'd tumbled into an unwise infatuation with a woman who had nothing to give him.

'He watches you all the time, although it's obvious he'd rather do almost anything else,' Clay told her, that swift, cold detachment hardening his voice.

Natalia compressed her lips. She didn't want Clay taking a dislike to Phil; jobs like his were scarce around Bowden. 'He'll get over it,' she hedged.

Picking up a spoon, she stirred her coffee, watching the creamy liquid swirl in fragrant spirals. Clay drank his black and sugarless.

'Is he stalking you?'

'No!' She controlled a lurch of shock. 'Of course he's not—in fact, until we saw him in your shed I hadn't seen him for ages. I don't know why he's behaving like this.'

'I understand why, poor devil,' Clay said evenly, his eyes kindling again as they met Natalia's. He gave her a narrow, enigmatic smile. 'Because you're a woman no man could forget—you have the power to eat into his heart and take over his brain.'

Natalia drew in a jagged, heavy breath, shaking her head. 'You make me sound like some—like a witch.'

'Like a fairy woman,' he said harshly. 'Beautiful and perilous and fascinating, with eyes that challenge and a mouth that allures and promises and seduces.'

She was still shaking her head when he looked across the room in unspoken summons, and was rewarded by the appearance of the waitress. 'We'll have the bill now, thank you,' he said pleasantly.

Smiling, the woman disappeared; in the background Soshanna's skilful fingers coaxed more—and thankfully different—romantic mood music from the piano, a slow, seductive air sizzling with an undercurrent of passion. Natalia looked blindly down at the white tablecloth, her mind blundering around and around, the sound of his voice echoing in her ears, her heart clenched in bitter pain.

Because he'd spoken only of desire, of need and hunger and passion, and although she wanted to experience them all with him, she wanted so much more now.

And that, she thought emptily, was ridiculous; how could you fall in love with a stranger in a few days?

'All right?' Clay's voice cut out everything else in the room, warming her, enclosing her, imprisoning her.

'Fine, thank you.' She picked up her coffee cup.

The coffee tasted bitter, but it gave her some sort of courage. Almost as soon as she set her cup down for the last time the bill appeared and was dealt with. As they stood up to go Clay looked deliberately over Natalia's head; after a moment of eye contact he gave a quick nod. Natalia didn't have to be a mind-reader to decipher the silent exchange. He'd just given Phil a keep-off sign.

Outside she could feel the clouds pressing down, weighted with rain. The forecast hadn't been good; neither she nor Clay had to worry about shifting cattle to higher ground, but the farmers on the flats would already have done so.

In the car he was silent until just before the turn-off; he switched on the wipers as a thin rain sifted down and smeared the windscreen. Then he said, 'Stay with me to-night, Natalia.'

'No,' she said steadily, wincing at the amount of discipline needed to get that one word out.

With headlights on full, a cattle truck surged around the next corner, veering too close. Natalia gasped, but Clay's strong hands held the wheel on course as the BMW's tyres bit into loose stones on the edge of the tarseal. The truck swung ponderously back on to the right side of the road and flashed past, swallowed by the night.

A signpost flicked yellow in the glare of the headlights. Smoothly Clay applied the brakes, and when the BMW had slowed sufficiently he turned the wheel and the big car left the sealed road and hit the first lot of potholes. This behemoth took each hole in its stride, whereas Natalia's truck rabbited through them with bone-shaking jolts.

'I'll do the gate,' she said when they turned off the road.

'Stay where you are,' he said curtly, and got out, a tall, dominating silhouette, moving with a lithe grace that sent a shiver the length of Natalia's spine. The rain shimmered down, crystal needles slanting across the beam of the lights. Clay heaved the gate off the drive and headed back for the car.

'Leave it open on your way out,' she said when he got in. 'There's nothing in this paddock. I shut the gate for the same reason I leave a light on in the house—because it looks as though I'm home.'

'Sensible of you,' he said levelly.

Good, he wasn't going to pressure her to sleep with him. Disappointment warred with relief, and won. She was, she realised with alarm, not just disappointed; her complicated mixture of emotions ranged from frustration through anger to outrage. She wanted him to kiss her into stupidity, to take the choice from her, to woo her with sex until she couldn't say no. Her body ached with a keening hunger that almost shut down her brain.

Not quite, thank God.

Outside the house he cut the engine. 'I'll walk you in.'

'Don't worry. No one is going to leap at me from the bushes. You'll only get wet.'

But of course he came with her, and at the back door he said her name, and when she looked up, knowing what was coming, unable to resist—feverishly delighted because she didn't want to resist—he kissed her and she went up in flames.

It was like that—fire and more fire—until all she could feel was the pressure of his mouth on hers, wild and demanding and making no compromises, calling something from her that had never existed before, a piercing desire, a need so acute she longed desperately to abandon herself to it.

Eventually he lifted his head, and his mouth moved to her eyelids, and then down the long line of her throat, finding the hurried pulse at its base. 'You smell of Natalia,' he said thickly against her skin, 'and you feel like paradise.'

Each word was a kiss, an incitement to surrender, a brand of possession; heat gathered inside her, insistent, merciless. She whispered his name, and of course he heard it.

'Let me come in with you,' he said deeply.

Her breath shuddered through her as she lifted weighted eyelids. His eyes glittered in a face drawn with need, harshly angular, and his ardent mouth seduced her with kisses that sabotaged her will-power, promising her heaven in the honey-eyed oblivion of the senses.

Exultant, consumed by pleasure, she almost yielded, but some last remnant of caution warned her in time. 'No,' she breathed. And more strongly, 'No, Clay.'

His arms tightened around her; he was fully aroused, as aroused as she was. Passion sharpened its claws on her; afraid she was losing the battle, she repeated, 'No, Clay!' She clenched her teeth to stop them chattering; her lips were tender, slightly swollen, making a meal of each word.

'It's all right,' he said in a raw voice, 'I'm not going to push you, or dog you. I'll go now—but I'll wait until you've checked the house out. Can I do the hydroponics for you?'

'No—'

'It can't be difficult,' he interrupted.

This, she thought dimly, was the difference between Clay and Dean Jamieson—Clay was protective, he wanted to save her from going out into the rain and the dark. His consideration warmed her heart and she said, 'It's not difficult at all,' and told him what to do: a matter of reading two dials.

He kissed her one last time, then set her away from him. In a thick, constricted tone he said, 'Go in now. Make sure everything's all right in the house, and come back here to tell me. Then I'll do the hydroponics and go straight home. I don't trust myself to come inside.'

Natalia didn't trust herself to answer. Without looking at him she pushed open the door, slipped in and closed it behind her. The chain pushed over, she stooped to remove her damp shoes and put them on the mat to dry.

When she straightened the blood ran to her head. Staggering slightly, she walked through the house checking each dark room, then went back to the door and opened it on the chain. 'Everything's fine,' she said to the still, frighteningly intent man on the other side.

'Goodnight.'

Calm down, she ordered her racing heart as she closed and locked the door. She was no blushing virgin, although it had happened so long ago she'd almost forgotten what it had been like except that because it had been the first time for both of them it had been clumsy and sweet and soon over.

Her mother had just died, and it had been obvious her father needed her to work the tunnel-houses with him. She'd made love with her boyfriend almost in a spirit of renunciation, of despair, because although they'd made plans to marry she'd known she'd have no future with him.

High drama, she thought with a twisted smile as she looked at her watch. And although she'd thought her heart was broken, she'd recovered. So had he.

The swift staccato of another sudden downpour on the iron roof accompanied her to her bedroom. In the darkness she saw the lights of Clay's car burn down the drive and swing up the road.

Turning away, she went into the bathroom and removed her make-up. She'd stopped shivering but her hands still trembled, and the tumult Clay's mouth had kindled in her still raced through her body. In the mirror her eyes glittered and she looked untamed, a creature from a primitive time, uncontrolled and passionate.

Her breath hissed out. How could it happen like that? Instant attraction was one thing—eventually it would have faded and died. But that...that wild urgency, that helpless, greedy appetite—that was terrifying. She'd been lost to everything but her ferociously carnal appetite for the man who had kissed her with such spellbinding intensity.

Later, before she slid into a restless sleep, she wondered if her mother had felt like that about her father.

And whether that appetite had anything to do with love.

CHAPTER SEVEN

A SHRILL, insistent burr cut through her sleep like a buzz-saw. Drugged, bewildered, Natalia groped for the alarm; it took her a moment or two to realise that the noise was the telephone. Muttering, she staggered out of her bed and into the kitchen, her eyes rapidly accustoming themselves to the dark as she picked up the receiver.

'Are you all right?' Clay demanded harshly.

'Yes.' The word was thick and clumsy in her mouth. 'What time is it?'

'Just after eleven. Have you got any lights on?'

'No.' Her brain refused to function. 'Why?'

'Don't turn any on. What's that noise?'

Another sound was clamouring through the chilly air. 'It's the alarm in the bedroom,' she told him. 'I have to check the hydroponics now.'

'Don't go outside,' Clay commanded urgently. 'Have you heard anything—any sounds outside?'

Shivering, she stared at the curtains. 'No.'

'I'll be down as soon as I can. Don't set foot outside the house and don't respond to anything until you hear me. I'll knock, then call you "Natalia, darling". Meantime, if any-one tries to get in—or if you hear anything unusual—ring me immediately.' He gave her the number, made her repeat it, then hung up.

By then adrenaline had pumped through her body, fully alerting it to some sort of emergency. Natalia pressed a hand to her hammering heart before racing back into her bed-room. Whatever was going on, she needed to be fully dressed. She did it by feel, dragging on jeans and a shirt and jersey, stuffing her feet into socks, her ears straining as she tucked her clothes in. Wide-eyed in the oppressive darkness, large torch in hand, she tiptoed to the laundry and got into her work boots.

A car swung into the gateway, its headlights sending out two cones of brilliance as it eased along the drive. Her breath locking in her chest, Natalia listened.

'Natalia, darling!' Clay's voice just reached her ears, but his knock was firm and unhurried.

Weak with relief, she opened the door. 'What's going on?' she asked, holding out a hand to pull him inside.

'I've been burgled,' he told her, coming in with a smooth, silent speed and closing the door behind him. 'I woke and heard a truck go down the hill. I wondered if they'd called in here before they came up to Pukekahu. Or on the way back.' Enough light came through the uncurtained window to reveal his face, hard-edged and purposeful.

'I haven't heard anything, and anyway, I've got nothing anyone would want.' She touched his arm in silent concern. It was like touching iron. 'What did they take?'

'Most of the pile of fencing materials by the road,' he said briefly. 'Some stuff's gone from the workshop too.'

Natalia repressed a craven shiver at the thought of thieves close by. 'I'll check the shed,' she said immediately.

'You'll do no such thing. I'll do it—'

'This is my place. I'll come with you.'

He crowded her back against the wall, his eyes gleaming with a feral heat, the scar suddenly livid down his face. 'Damn you,' he said in a low growl, 'you push and push and push—Natalia, you're asking for trouble.'

The kiss was fast and punishing, and she kissed him back just as fiercely, moulding her mouth to his, holding his head down with a hand clenched in his black hair. Yet the touch of his mouth transformed her aggression into passion, and when he at last lifted his head she was shaking, her face flushed and her mouth as subtly swollen as his, her eyes drowsy and smouldering.

'You're going to drive me mad,' he said with something

like satisfaction in his tone. 'Stay here, please. I'll worry about you if you come with me.'

'If you heard them drive down the hill they're long gone. Anyway, I'll be frantic if you go out there by yourself.'

He looked at her with narrowed, darkened eyes. She thought she saw the flicker of a muscle in his jaw and braced herself for further argument, but he astounded her by saying, 'All right. Hold out your hand.'

Bemused, she obeyed. Something cold was pressed into it. 'The car key,' he said briefly. 'If anything happens, use it to get away. Promise?'

'Promise.' But she crossed the fingers of her free hand.

Clay switched off the light then opened the door and went out ahead of her into the dark, stopping on the doorstep until he was convinced there was nothing out there.

'Move as quietly as you can,' he said almost noiselessly.

Nodding, she followed, trying to walk as silently as he did—creepily aware of the huge darkness and the trees, the many hiding places. At least the rain had stopped, and the elusive light from a hidden moon revealed enough of the path so that they didn't stumble.

Although the toolshed door gaped open, the momentary gleam of Clay's torch revealed that nothing had gone. 'I'll put that padlock on tomorrow, nevertheless,' he said beneath his breath. 'Where's the hydroponics computer?'

'In the first tunnel-house,' she answered, sudden fear tightening her voice.

A big hand squeezed hers. 'It'll be all right,' he said.

But it wasn't. The thieves had wrenched the equipment free, cut the plastic pipes and taken her father's expensive, state-of-the-art computer system. Not content with that, they'd rampaged silently through the tunnel-houses and slashed every capsicum plant off at ground level.

Staring around at the wreckage, Natalia said dully, 'Well, that's that, then.'

'What?'

'Nothing's insured, and I can't afford...' She let the

words trail away and turned aimlessly. 'I wonder why they wanted it. And why they destroyed the plants.'

'They can sell the computer system,' he said savagely, pulling her into the heat and the strength of his body, holding her there as his cheek came down on the top of her head. 'Or use it on a cannabis plantation. As for the rest— mindless vandalism. All I can think of is that you might have come out here while they were doing this. Get a toothbrush and we'll go to Pukekahu.'

She shook her head, but his arms tightened until she could barely breathe and he said violently, 'I'm not leaving you here, Natalia, so you have two choices. I stay here with you, or you come with me. Which will it be?'

His fierce grip relaxed as she lifted her head. In the ghostly light of the ruined tunnel-house, she made out the outline of his face; the determined features wavered and blurred as she drew a shallow, ragged breath. 'I don't care,' she said, surrendering to a will far stronger than hers.

'You're coming with me,' he told her, and released her, but kept a hand at her back as he urged her out of the tunnel-house. They were halfway along the muddy path to the house when she stopped.

'What?' he asked soundlessly.

'The cattle—and the hens. I have to check them.'

He was a farmer, so he didn't object. And this time when they walked he kept her beside him, her hand in his. Nevertheless, he didn't use his torch until they got to the henhouse; its beam revealed the hens perched safely, gazing sleepily down.

'They're all right,' she muttered.

But the paddock where the cattle had been was empty. Dry-eyed, Natalia bit her lip to hold back a sob as Clay swore beside her.

His arm came around her shoulders; holding her as though she might fall, he said, 'Did you see anything of the truck that almost hit us on the main road?'

'No.' She'd been too focused on him to notice anything more than the sides of the truck.

'They came twice, the bastards,' he said with such cold fury that her heart quailed. 'First for the cattle, then the fencing materials. A lucrative night's work. Are you all right?'

'Yes.' What else could she say? No, my whole life is crumbling around my ears, because now the Ogilvies are going to miss out on the comfortable retirement they deserve?

'Then let's go. The police should be at Pukekahu by now.'

At the house he waited while Natalia got a sponge bag and pyjamas and a change of clothes, then took her to the car.

When she sat huddled in the seat, Clay leaned over and pulled her seat belt across her, clicking it in. 'Don't worry,' he said, his voice deep and sure and confident, 'it won't look so bad tomorrow.'

Natalia didn't say anything. If she opened her mouth she'd probably howl like a banshee.

A police car had drawn up at the gate of Pukekahu homestead. Stiffening her shoulders, Natalia got out and walked beside Clay over to the constable who stood outside it.

She was a stranger to Natalia. Brisk, calm, businesslike, she interviewed them both, then said, 'I'll get back to you as soon as there's any news.' She looked at Natalia. 'Are you all right? You look pale.'

'I'm fine,' Natalia said.

'She'll stay here for rest of the night,' Clay said.

The policewoman nodded as she got into the car. 'They're not likely to come back, so get a decent sleep.'

The white car turned and disappeared down the road. 'Where's Phil?' Natalia asked quietly.

'I presume he's spending the night with his girlfriend.' Clay said crisply. 'Come on inside. I don't like that alarming docility.'

Natalia couldn't summon a snappy answer. She felt as though something had broken inside her.

The last three years had all been in vain. Even when she'd sold Xanadu and everything else the Ogilvies would have to kiss goodbye to most of the money they'd saved for their retirement fund.

Because of her charming, lovable, irresponsible father.

At the foot of the long flight of steps on to the verandah she stopped, exhausted. Clay scooped her into his arms and strode up, his boots barely making a sound on the wet wood.

She didn't protest. Tomorrow she'd deal with everything, but for the moment she was grateful for his decisiveness. With a small sigh of relief she relaxed into his arms, resting her head against his hard shoulder as the jasmine flowers teased her nostrils with their potent musky scent.

'My mother would have cut that jasmine out,' she murmured. 'She said it was a terrible, grasping, greedy weed. My father adored it.'

'It's beautiful and it's tough—a survivor,' he said evenly. 'Like you, Natalia.'

She didn't feel like a survivor. She said tonelessly, 'I'm not capable of holding myself up at the moment, much less a house. This is such a lovely old place; it was wicked to let it go to rack and ruin.'

'Did you know the previous owner?'

'Not very well.' And it wasn't a lie. She'd only known—and been deceived by—the persona Dean Jamieson presented to the world: a lying, laughing mask. Compared to Clay, Dean was a shallow excuse for a man. She tacked on, 'He's a South Islander.'

Clay set her down on her feet. Although one arm stayed around her while he unlocked the door, she felt his withdrawal, as palpable as the cold winds of winter. Even his voice was remote when he asked, 'Can you walk?'

'Of course I can.' Never mind that her legs felt as though they'd been stuffed with cotton wool.

'All right?' Clay asked abruptly as the lights flared. He

closed the door, locked it, and pulled the curtains to cover it.

She looked up at him, meeting narrowed, intent eyes; the mouth she'd kissed so passionately was a thin line.

Unconsciously she straightened her spine. 'Yes, thank you. Where am I going to sleep?'

'In my bed. I'll sleep on the sofa.'

She didn't realise she'd sighed until he smiled, a humourless, violent smile.

'You really don't think much of the male sex, do you?' he asked with an inflection that iced her through to the marrow. 'You're shocked and worried—what sort of man would I be to persuade you into making love?' He touched her mouth, then dropped his hand to rest a fingertip on the hurried tumbling pulse at the base of her throat.

The same sort of man as Dean, she thought as the caress drove the breath from her lungs.

With dilating eyes she gazed up while Clay's fingers curved around her throat, warm, commanding, possessive. In a voice that was deep and potent and sensual he finished, 'But it's going to happen, Natalia, because we both want it.'

It was a simple statement of fact, cool, authoritative. Mesmerised by the compelling heat of his gaze, the subtle fetter of his hand on her skin and the wild tumult that it aroused, Natalia said unevenly, 'Not yet.'

Something darkened his eyes, something molten and wholly primitive, but the thick black lashes hid his emotions, and when they lifted again he was once more fully in control.

'Not tonight,' he corrected. 'Do you want a drink before you go to bed?'

Natalia shook her head. 'I'm tired,' she said jerkily. 'I'll sleep on the sofa, though. It's not big enough for you.'

'My bed is comfortable,' he said. 'The bedroom isn't anything much, but it's dry and reasonably warm. I'll be fine out here.'

Her brows met. Through her teeth she said, 'Don't you ever compromise? I'll sleep on the sofa, Clay.'

His laughter, soft and mocking, exasperated her.

'I don't think I've ever met anyone who compromised as little as you,' he drawled, 'but if it makes you feel better, sleep out here. I'll get some sheets and a duvet.'

'You've got a spare? Good. But you don't need to make up the sofa—I'll do it.'

He said from very close behind her, 'I've compromised, Natalia, now it's your turn. Go and wash your face or clean your teeth or do whatever you need to do in the bathroom.'

Some hard, braced part of her dissolved, yielded. 'All right,' she said wearily. 'Where is it?'

'Through here.'

Huge, cold and damp, the bathroom was entirely unwelcoming. Natalia bit her lip as she looked around. It didn't seem possible that Clay should be camping out in quarters like this. Then she thought of the boy who'd left an unwelcoming home when he was sixteen and made his own way in the world. Legacy or not, he'd probably endured more squalor than this.

Back in the sitting room he'd made up a bed on the sofa, and very comfortable it looked, with two pillows and a thick white duvet. Tiredness born of shock washed over Natalia, weighing down her bones and her eyelids.

'Are you sure you'll be warm enough?' Clay asked, frowning. 'I'll leave the heater on just in case.'

'You don't need to—I'm used to sleeping in a cold room.' Her face split in a yawn.

He laughed quietly. 'Then goodnight, Natalia. If you need me during the night, my bedroom's directly opposite the bathroom.'

'Goodnight, Clay.' The words were heavy, almost slurred as exhaustion caught her in its lazy, inexorable grip.

Once he'd gone she changed into her pyjamas and turned the lights off. Snuggling under the duvet and sheet, she managed two thoughts before sleep claimed her—she didn't have to get up and check the hydroponics system, and her bedclothes smelt faintly of Clay.

Some time later in this interminable night she woke, gripped by a nameless dread. Hardly breathing, she angled her head and searched the darkness.

Yes, that was it.

A light rattle against the French window, like someone trying a handle, or perhaps seeing if anyone inside responded.

Although the clouds pressed low, that vagrant moon lent enough light for her to make out a dark silhouette through the thin curtains.

Fright and fury in equal components gave her speed and silence; she wriggled from the warm nest of bedclothes and inched her way across the door to the rest of the house. Easing it barely open, she slipped through it and groped down the hall. She hadn't taken more than one step inside Clay's room when he said in a barely audible voice, 'Natalia.'

Low-voiced, she told him, 'There's someone trying to get in through the French windows.'

She didn't hear him move, but when he spoke next he was much closer. 'Stay here,' he breathed. 'And I mean it— I don't want to have to worry about you. Here's my cellphone—if anything happens to me get the hell out of here and ring the emergency number.' His hand found her shoulder, slid the length of her arm, and wrapped her fingers around the phone. 'Stay here,' he repeated fiercely.

Shivering, she sat down on the bed, her nervous fingers pleating the bedcover; after several moments she realised exactly what it was beneath her hand. Frowning, she explored further. Clay's bed was covered only by what seemed to be a coat.

She bit her lip; he'd stripped the sheets and duvet for her. Oh, why hadn't she thought of that? In spite of that elegant sitting room, he was only camping in the homestead—of course he wouldn't have extra bedding.

She'd deal with that later. Getting up, she tiptoed to the bedroom door and listened. A sudden blinding flood of light through one of the bedroom windows made her wince, but with it came relief. Clay wouldn't have turned on the verandah light unless he knew—and trusted—the person at the door.

Nothing moved out there, but she could hear the low grumble of two men speaking. Breathlessly she eased down the hall, stopping just outside the door to the sitting room. Clay hadn't switched the light on in the room.

'...see you tomorrow morning,' he said abruptly.

The click of the French door followed; she heard someone tramping along the verandah and down the steps, and the sound of a car engine. A moment later the verandah light died, and darkness enveloped her again.

Pushing the door open, she said, 'He must have tiptoed along the verandah. I would have heard him otherwise.'

In a voice rigid with anger, Clay said, 'I told you to stay out of this.'

'It was Phil, wasn't it?'

'Yes.'

She stepped into the room, her heart banging with unnecessary fuss. 'What was he doing here?'

Clay said, 'Looking for you, poor devil.'

'What do you mean?' Natalia asked stupidly, stretching her eyes wide open to search the darkened room for him. 'How did he know I wasn't at home?'

'He saw that the fencing had gone, so he raced back to make sure you were all right. When he realised you weren't there he came here.' He spoke almost indifferently.

'Why would he do that?'

'Because he assumed you'd be sleeping with me, I presume,' he answered on a cool, judicial note.

Frowning, she said, 'It seems odd. What did you tell him?'

'The truth. That when you realised the capsicums had been vandalised you decided to spend the night here.' He spoke evenly, yet there were undercurrents in his voice, in his words—undercurrents she was too tired to decipher.

He went on, 'If Phil *is* stalking you, I want to know so that I can do something about it.'

'Clay, I'm really not up to melodrama in the middle of the night.' Her voice wavered. 'Of course Phil's not stalking me. I told you, I hadn't seen him for weeks until you came.'

'And showed my interest so openly that the news must have been around the district by lunchtime the next day.'

Natalia shook her head. 'Phil's not like that.' Sudden, furious tears stung her eyes. 'Oh, *why* did you have to come here? We were all fine before you arrived in Bowden.'

His laughter grated. 'Were you? Get back to bed, I'll sort it out in the morning.'

Chagrined, she fought back her humiliating weepiness. 'I didn't realise you'd taken the duvet off your bed for me. It's much warmer here than in your room—you take the duvet and give me the coat, or whatever it is you've got on your bed.'

Charged with tension, the silence raised each tiny hair on her skin. Then he said quietly, 'Natalia, will you please just shut up?'

'But—'

'Because all I can think of is you under me, and no sleep for either of us during the rest of the night.'

Her heart slammed in her chest. Shakily, stupidly, she said, 'That's all I can think of too.'

After a taut moment he said in an almost soundless voice, 'Are you scared of me?'

'No.' If she had any sense of self-preservation she'd be running—but then, if she had any sense of self-preservation she'd never have given him the opening.

He said, 'You can just sleep with me if you want to, without making love.'

Because he couldn't see her, she let her lips stretch in a painful travesty of a smile. 'Do you think that's possible?'

Another silence, until he said with silky precision, 'I could try.'

'I don't want you to.' Natalia turned eagerly into the arms that caught her and pulled her against his lean strength. Her quick hands slipped across the coiled, tense muscles of his bare shoulders to link around his neck as she lifted her head for his kiss.

After the hungry need of the last one, she was surprised when his mouth touched hers with tender attention, the primitive urgency leashed. For the moment, she thought. Only for the moment...

And then the moment was over, and she was lost in a heady desire that stripped every civilised response from her, leaving her captive to a wildfire sexuality sprung from some unknown source. Using only the language of the senses, Clay demanded surrender, and she met his demand with her own, pressing herself against him with an imperative craving that should have shocked her. It didn't—nothing could shock her now.

A rough noise caught in his throat. Natalia opened her mouth to his, taking as he took, exploring as he explored. Driving need burned away the last barriers—the ones she hadn't even known existed—until all she could feel, all she could taste, all she could smell was Clay.

How long was it before he broke the kiss? She didn't know, but her murmured protest brought a low, breathy laugh from him. 'I could spend all night kissing you like this, but let's go to bed first,' he said.

'Yes.'

From that first meeting he'd challenged her with his virile masculine authority; now was the pay-off, and she wasn't going to retreat. Strangely, the destruction of everything she'd worked for these past years gave her the freedom to capitulate.

'I've ached for you ever since I saw you.' He gave a low, dangerous laugh. 'The first time I took you home I couldn't unlock your door because my hands were shaking.'

'Truly?' she asked huskily. 'I was so embarrassed, because mine were trembling.'

'I know. It gave me hope.'

'Of what?'

He laughed again. 'Of taking you on a huge bed with exotic hangings to match your beauty, on satin and silk and fur,' he said. 'The bed here is a very poor substitute.'

'It's yours; that's all that matters.' Her acceptant hands slipped to narrow male hips covered only by thin cotton.

He said, 'You deserve pearls to caress that ivory skin, emeralds as brilliant as your eyes, but I can only offer you a bed in a tumbledown house that—'

'Clay, I want you—just you,' she interrupted swiftly. His unusual diffidence startled her—and pleased her as much as his admission of wanting her, of aching for her. It made them equal, because she too had lain awake at night, an unwilling captive to the crazy, erotic dreams of passion.

Scooping the duvet and the sheets from the sofa, he said, 'Bring the pillows.'

Natalia picked them up; together she and Clay walked through the damp chill of the hallway to his bedroom, cool also, and with the faint musty scent of all old, neglected houses.

Once in the bedroom he switched on the lamp beside the bed. Her gaze flew to the dressing gown spread out across the bed; she said huskily, 'You must have been freezing.'

'The thought of you curled up on my sofa was enough to keep me warm.' His voice deepened, softened. 'Hot.'

Apart from the black boxer shorts, he was naked. Clutching the pillows, Natalia stared at him with eyes that widened as they scanned his face, his chest and shoulders, gleaming gold in the lamplight, and the long, heavily muscled legs. She swallowed. 'I doubt it.'

'Believe it,' he said. 'But you're shivering.'

'It's not from the cold.'

Laughing low in his throat, he pulled the dressing gown off the bed. Natalia dumped the pillows and took the edge of the sheet he flicked out across the bed. Her hands shook as she helped him. The mundane task should have eased some of the tension, but she found herself indulging in a fleeting, wistful fantasy where they did this each morning…

Enough of that, she told herself caustically. This house—this room—might be old and damp and as bare as hers, but there was an enormous difference between Clay Beauchamp and a woman who had just lost everything.

For a moment her hands stilled. Then she set her jaw and straightened the duvet.

Across the too-personal expanse of bed he looked at her. The lamp picked out the angular framework of his face, touched with a loving light the darkly gold skin, the shimmering eyes, the black brows and heavy lashes, the hard, chiselled mouth, the cleft in his chin, and the thin pale line of the scar.

He said, 'I suppose every lover you've had has told you how beautiful you are.'

'Have all your lovers told you how magnificent you are?' Natalia didn't try to hide the snap in her words; she hated the thought of any other women who had looked at him with eyes as covetous as hers.

His brows lifted. 'An occasional one,' he admitted. 'Shall we start again? When I first saw you I thought you were the most exciting woman I'd ever seen.' His mouth tilted into a lopsided smile. 'I haven't changed my mind.'

Stomach clenching, Natalia watched him walk around towards her.

'You light up my world,' he said with ragged emphasis. His hands closed on her shoulders, turning her so that she faced away from him. Against her tingling neck his mouth was possessive, as possessive as the hands that moved to the button on her pyjamas. 'I won't hurt you, Natalia,' he said while the buttons fell open.

She was only just realising how much he could hurt her. And that it was too late to change her mind now, too late to be sensible—even if she wanted to be.

'I know,' she said. Her voice sounded thin and unsure and stupidly young. 'Clay, I haven't—I'm not protected.'

'It's all right.' Unwillingly she looked down, trembling at the tawny male hands that cupped her breasts as though they were rare and precious to him. The tantalising contrast between their callused warmth and the chill air across her pale skin twisted a knot of excitement deep inside her.

'Tell me now if a condom's not enough,' he said, a jagged note beneath the words exciting her.

Condoms were not infallible; there was a chance of pregnancy, and even now he was giving her the opportunity to turn back. How different from Dean Jamieson's greedy desire...

Clay's child. Natalia froze, then relaxed. 'It's enough.' Two words, but they spelled surrender and hope and an unspoken commitment.

'Then turn to me.'

Helplessly, a prisoner of the rising tide of passion, she swivelled in his arms, somehow ending up without her pyjama jacket. His eyes were narrowed and crystalline, a dusky flush outlining the bold sweep of his cheekbones as his gaze smouldered over her.

She curbed her instinctive attempt to hide what he had exposed. Although colour flamed from her breasts to her face she held her head high.

'''But beauty's self she is, When all her robes are gone.''' he quoted in an impeded voice, his arms contracting around her, his faint, elemental male scent overwhelming her.

As hunger tore the last fragment of common sense free, whirling it along the current of passion like a leaf in a flood, Natalia shuddered, abandoned to a sensuous magic she'd never known before.

CHAPTER EIGHT

KISSING her deeply, Clay picked her up and lifted her into
the bed; she gasped at the chill of the sheets against her
back, and shut her eyes as strong hands slid her pyjama
bottoms down. A moment later he was naked beside her,
holding her in his arms, his mouth buried in her hair.

Then he kissed her throat, and while she was still shaking
at the splendour of his lips on her skin he began to suckle
at her breast.

She heard herself moan, heard the catch in his breathing,
braced herself against the drumming of her heart in her ears.
Behind her closed lids darkness surrounded her like a lover,
intensifying each sensation, focusing her entirely on the sensuous torment of his mouth.

Lax, boneless, she whispered, 'Too much.'

'Not enough.' His breath washed over the moistened,
acutely sensitive areola. 'I don't think I'll ever get enough
of you. I like being touched too, Natalia.'

She pressed her palm above his heart, exulting at the uneven thunder against it. Did she do that to him, or would it
beat so erratically, so fiercely, for any woman?

Probably, she thought, trying to retain some remnant of
intelligence. Why should she think she was special amongst
his lovers? Of course he'd said so—and for this night, this
moment, she'd believe him.

Forcing her eyes slightly open, she traced the arrogant
line of his jawbone—rough silk beneath her fingertips—the
cord of his neck, the iron flex and curve of his upper arm,
the soft tuft in his armpit, the tiny points of his nipples,
while the insistent tug of his mouth ravished her into another
plane of existence where all she could do was feel.

'That's enough,' he growled suddenly, and when she froze he added with brutal directness, 'I overestimated my self-control. When you look at me so ravenously from those slanted green eyes it goes out the window. All I want to do is bury myself in you and lose myself there.'

One lean, knowledgeable hand slid to her hip, and then to the small indentation of her navel; astonished, Natalia discovered that it too was sensitive, with a direct line to her innermost core. His hand was sure and gentle, relentless, inexorable, his mouth equally searching and unsparing.

Twisting beneath his primal ravishment, she touched him as he touched her, until he caught her hands in one of his and pulled them above her head, anchoring them to the pillow. 'Wait,' he said, and then he moved over her.

Natalia was ready—she knew she was ready: her every pulse clamorous and urgent, her body already slick with anticipation—but for a moment her breath stilled in her throat. Straining upwards, her hips thrust against his, seeking, yearning, demanding the strength and power there.

'Yes,' he said between his teeth, and drove home, filling her, consuming her, uniting with her in the most primitive of all embraces.

She said his name, her voice high and stark and compulsive, and he withdrew slightly before driving home again, establishing a rhythm, slow at first and then—as they began to spin together in the ecstatic, merciless dance of the senses—faster and faster, until at last she was hurled by unbearable pleasure into some rapturous world where all that mattered was Clay and this violent, stormy enchantment.

He followed her immediately, flinging his head back, his breathing harsh as his arms tightened around her and he too reached a shuddering climax.

With the waves of her own peak still shimmering through her, Natalia lay spread beneath him in voluptuous abandon, her lungs pumping breath into her, the thudding of her heart gradually easing. Sweaty, sated, she wondered hazily whether life held anything more.

Eventually Clay moved. She murmured, and he said, 'It's all right, I'm not going away.'

Taking her with him, he rolled over and tucked her into his side with her cheek on his shoulder. Too exhausted to speak, she kissed the skin there. His chest expanded, and he laughed as he took her chin in his hand and tipped her face upwards.

'So those eyes *are* natural—no green contact lenses,' he said drily.

Why had she thought that making love would have the same effect on him as it did on her?

'No contact lenses,' she said, seeking out the cleft in his chin with a lazy forefinger. 'My eyes are the same colour as my father's.'

'Did you get those seductive eyelids from him too?' He kissed her lashes closed.

'No, they're my mother's.'

Her body stirred, and the remorseless tides of hunger and desire began to pulse once more as his mouth roved her face.

But Clay pulled away, put out an arm and turned off the lamp. 'Sleep now,' he commanded quietly.

Natalia woke to an empty room and the sound of voices on the verandah. Clay—and Phil. On the end of the bed were the clothes she'd packed so quickly the previous night.

It seemed weeks ago.

Hastily, stealthily, she got out of bed and into the jeans and shirt, wincing at the tell-tale stiffness of muscles rarely used. The voices faded, and she wondered whether she should just leave—slip down the road and set about organising her affairs.

No, pride forbade it. She wasn't ashamed of making love with Clay and she wasn't going to sneak off as though she'd done something humiliating or illegal. After pulling the bedclothes back to air, she cleaned her teeth and washed her face in the chilly bathroom, then returned to the bedroom to make the bed.

She was standing at the window, one finger tracing the cracked lines of paint, when Clay said from the door, 'You can come out now. He's gone.'

'Phil?'

'Yes.' He didn't look like the lover of the night before; his face was grim and the bones stood out prominently. 'I sent him into Bowden. Do you want some breakfast?'

'No, thank you,' she said. 'I need to get back home.'

'I'll take you.'

Without looking at him, she nodded, picked up the parcel she'd made of her discarded clothes and walked towards the door. He didn't move; she stopped, and looked up into an unyielding face.

'Having second thoughts?' he asked.

'It's too late for that.'

'Far too late.' Anger prowled a second in the golden depths of his eyes, was banished. He bent and kissed her, hard and fiercely, a brand on her mouth, staking a claim. 'It's done now,' he said. 'I sent Phil away because I knew you wouldn't want him to find you here, but I don't care who knows that we're lovers.'

'Neither do I.' It was almost true.

A lean finger lifted her chin. 'Don't worry about anything,' he said.

How easy for him to say that! Her lashes drooped.

'And don't look at me like that unless you want to find yourself back in that bed,' he said, his mouth compressing.

Her startled glance brought a humourless laugh. 'No, I thought not,' he said obliquely. 'We've got a fair amount to do today. Let's go.'

In the car she asked, 'Have you heard from the police yet?'

'No.' He steered down the road, hands steady, confident on the wheel. 'What are your plans?'

After one famished look Natalia kept her eyes well away from those hands. Her skin still sang to their mastery, glowing at the memory.

She said stonily, 'I'll have to ring Mr and Mrs Ogilvie—the people who hold the mortgage—and tell them what's happened.'

'And then?'

'I'll see if I can organise another loan.'

'You won't,' he said brutally.

'I know, but I have to try.'

After a short silence he said, 'Yes, I suppose you do.'

'If I can't, I'll sell Xanadu, pay the Ogilvies what I can, and then I presume I'll have to file for bankruptcy.' Her voice lacked emotion. 'Do you still want to buy the place?'

'It depends on the price,' he said laconically, 'and I imagine that will be set by the Ogilvies. They'll probably get someone in to value everything. Don't do anything for a few hours.'

'What difference will a few hours make?'

'Exactly.' His tone gentled as he went on, 'You shouldn't have to go through this.'

'I'm young and strong,' she returned woodenly. 'It's not the end of the world.'

'Only the end of a dream.'

'Damn you, stop it,' she whispered.

The car turned into her gateway, rode the potholes and drew up outside the shed. In a cool, deliberate voice he said, 'It was never your dream, Natalia. What would you do if you had the choice? What *are* your dreams?'

Staring through the windscreen at the overgrown garden and a house that desperately needed paint, she said bleakly, 'I don't think I have any left.'

Silence lengthened until he finally said, 'I'm coming in with you.'

'Haven't you got things to do?'

'I'll help you work out what you can salvage.'

Her heart leapt. 'Thank you,' she said slowly.

He leaned over and turned her head, dropping another fierce kiss on her mouth. Her lips clung, and the kiss deepened. They were both breathing faster when he lifted his head. Eyes raking her face, he said, 'Soon you and I are going to stay in a bed all day.'

Hugging his words, because they meant he wanted some sort of future with her, she went into the house and dropped off her clothes, then fed the hens.

'Perhaps Liz's mother might want them,' Natalia said. 'She likes hens.'

'That sounds a good idea.' Clay closed the gate behind her and they walked back to the tunnel-houses.

Sick at heart, Natalia looked around the dying plants. The capsicums were limp, their dull leaves folding in on themselves. Fingering one glossy green fruit, she said, 'They'll be all right if I strip them now.'

'I'll help you.'

They ended up with several bins of second-grade fruit. 'What do you want done with these?' Clay asked as she picked up the last pepper.

'Sort them and pack them and send them off to the markets.' Carefully staring down at the smooth green skin, she hefted it in her hand. 'Clay, you don't need to stay. There's nothing for you to do here.'

'Then I'll see you in a couple of hours,' he said, and bent to kiss her. Against her mouth he said, 'Don't do anything final while I'm away.'

She pulled back. 'I have to get the peppers—'

'Anything about this financial mess of yours,' he qualified impatiently, eyes narrowing.

The pepper weighed heavily in her hand. For three years she'd cared for capsicums as though they were her children; she'd got used to the scent of them, used to the mess they made of her hands, accustomed to their smooth green blocky shape.

Now it was all over. 'All right,' she said at last.

She'd just returned from taking the cases down to catch

the carrier when she heard a car. Lithely she jumped down from the truck, her eyes lighting up as she saw Clay's BMW turn into the gateway.

He got out, long legs moving with deceptive ease as he came towards her, tawny eyes gleaming, hair black as night in the sun. They kissed, and this time he said, 'Mmm, you always smell so good. Warm and secret and sexy.'

'I smell like capsicums,' she said on a half-laugh, hugging him. 'Have you had lunch?'

'No. How are things?'

'The peppers are on their way to the markets, but I haven't had time to do anything else.'

'Good.' He turned her towards the house. 'Feed me and then we'll talk.'

She said sweetly, 'I won't feed you, but I'll provide the wherewithal for you to eat.'

He laughed. 'One day I'll show you how very erotic feeding someone can be,' he said, looking down at her with a disturbing intensity that sent a shiver through her.

They ate lettuce and some cold roast meat and a potato salad with a Russian dressing that had been her mother's favourite. Then she made tea while he rinsed the dishes, and they took their cups out on to the verandah.

Leaning against the balustrade, his cup lost in his hands, Clay surveyed her face.

In an expressionless voice he said, 'I'll buy the place from you as a going concern.'

She gazed blindly out over the neglected, unfertilised paddocks. 'You'd probably get it cheaper if I sold everything up,' she said remotely.

'It's unlikely.' Dark brows drew together. 'Buying Xanadu is a business decision, Natalia.'

She gave him a surprised look. 'I know.'

The midday sun lured hidden flames from his black head. Hard features hardened further, if that was possible, and his eyes were very steady and level, golden and predatory.

'My next offer isn't,' he said. 'I want to pay off the rest of the mortgage.'

Natalia shook her head, not letting herself feel. 'I can't let you do that,' she said uncompromisingly.

'Why not? I can afford it.'

'That's got nothing to do with it.' She spoke rapidly, brusquely, unable to deal with the emotions clawing at her. 'I couldn't accept it.'

He shrugged. 'I want to do it. And at least this way the Ogilvies will get their money.'

Oh, that was cruel! Tears stung her eyes as she turned away. 'Clay—please don't. I'd never be able to pay you back.' Painfully, her voice stiff with pride, she added, 'I'm not like my father.'

'Everyone in Bowden knows you're not like your father. There'd be no question of payment,' he said, his voice edged with something more than exasperation, 'if you were living with me.'

Until that moment Natalia hadn't understood what fantasies she'd been weaving, what hidden hopes had germinated in the depths of her heart. She'd said that she wasn't like her father, but she was, she was, because she too had begun to weave fantasies out of moonbeams.

Except that her dreams would harm no one but her.

Her head came up. 'I don't think I'm very good mistress material.'

'I don't want a mistress,' Clay said curtly.

That doomed hope flickered a little. 'Then what?'

He didn't hesitate or pause, but she got the impression that he was choosing his words with more than usual care, and when he spoke it was with a cool, inflexible logic that hurt because she didn't understand it. 'You need help—'

'I'd rather be your mistress than an object of pity,' she flashed, wounded in some exquisitely tender place and desperate to stop him from inflicting any more pain. Without giving him time to speak, she added curtly, 'At least I'd have some personal freedom if I were bankrupt.'

'Hardly. Do you know the terms for bankruptcy?' he asked roughly. 'You'd find them extremely restrictive.'

She shook her head. 'More restrictive than being your mistress? All I want is to be free,' she said angrily, because anger was easier to endure than the anguish that clawed her heart. 'Is that so hard to understand?'

'I do understand.' But his face was closed against her, his eyes opaque and hard, the mouth that had ravished her the previous night now an uncompromising line.

'Then why ask me to be your mistress?'

He snarled something below his breath before answering roughly, 'I said nothing about you being my mistress—you're the one who keeps tossing that word around. I want to pay your debt because you've had a bloody awful time and you've worked your heart out and this final straw is totally unfair! And because you'll never forgive yourself for not repaying the Ogilvies. I know you, Natalia—it will eat into your soul for the rest of your life.'

Keeping her eyes on the hens busily scratching their way through her newest bed of seedlings, she said wearily, 'But it's not your problem.'

He set his mug down on the balustrade and turned to follow her gaze, giving her the chance to feast her eyes on the width of his shoulders, the sheer male strength that had been tempered for her last night—and then unleashed in all its power. Her heart cramped, tightened, knotted in her chest.

How had it happened? How had she moved so swiftly, so secretly from acute awareness to fascination, and from there to this exultant, terrifying love?

And now Clay was tempting her with the promise of heaven.

But it was heaven with a sting in the tail, a paradise with poison at the heart of it. He offered her the rootless, carnal pleasure of desire when she longed for the hardy, tenacious plant of love, with its rare beauty and strength and commitment—love, with the resilience and determination of the jasmine that had kept Clay's homestead together, she thought bleakly.

'You *are* my problem,' he said, keeping his eyes on the sun-washed paddocks she'd tried to conserve. Levelly, without emotion, he went on, 'I can't bear to leave you in this mess. If you live with me, accept the money, you'll be free to go whenever you want to. You can make plans for the future, even go to university or art school if that's what you want.' His voice deepened as he turned her head and surveyed her face, the banked golden eyes alert and calculating. 'And free of paying for your father's pain and his mistakes. You'd hate it if the Ogilvies suffered because you were too proud to take the money.'

'I'd hate even more to live with the stigma of being paid for sex,' she retorted icily, furious at the moral blackmail.

Flames leapt in the dark gold of his eyes. 'If that's your take on it, then we'll say goodbye.'

She didn't—*couldn't*—move; the thought of seeing him go literally paralysed her.

In a calmly reasonable tone, Clay went on, 'Look at this logically. I can afford to pay the Ogilvies in full. You can't. And I want to pay your debts because you're important to me, not because I'm trying to buy you. If I thought you were for sale I wouldn't want you, Natalia.'

Struggling to find some answer to that, she bit her lip and looked away.

'On second thoughts,' he said curtly, 'perhaps logic has nothing to do with it.' In one lithe, silent movement he came away from the balustrade and tangled his hands in her hair and kissed her.

Natalia fought but it was no use; he used his great strength to subdue her, although not to hurt.

She should have bitten him, punched him in the solar plexus, kneed him. Instead she responded with a feverish intensity that was partly based on a baffled, frustrated anger, partly on the wildness he summoned in her, a need the previous night hadn't assuaged. Their tongues duelled, and then she gave up, surrendering with a low groan to the hunger that overwhelmed her.

'You're like a drug,' he muttered, his lips barely moving, his eyes glittering, 'all sweetness and passion and fury—I can't get enough of you. Whether you like it or not, Natalia, pride and stiff-necked resistance aren't going to keep us apart. Come and live with me and we'll set the world on fire.'

'And then?' she asked in a muffled voice.

His hand moved to her hip and held her against him. 'What do you want?'

Oh, just the world—to know that he loved her as she loved him. 'I don't know,' she said painfully. 'When you touch me I can't think.'

Shaking her head, she pulled back.

Although he let her go, he watched her through half-closed eyes. 'I wonder what it is about you that makes me forget everything I've ever learned about women? At first I thought it was your mouth...' he leaned down and kissed it with tormenting gentleness '...then that it was your eyes...' Two kisses sealed them. His voice had sunk to a deep smooth murmur, intensely erotic as his mouth roamed her face.

Against her cheek he said, 'Then I wondered if it was the texture and colour of your skin, ivory and pearls and magnolia flowers, all woman, all mystery. But I got sidetracked by your laugh, and the way you look when you're angry, and the way your mind works...' He smiled against her temple and finished, 'I think I'm fixated on you.'

Surely this was enough? He might not yet know it, but surely he loved her? And if he didn't, then perhaps he would learn to.

If she went with him.

Shivering, her heart thudding in her ears, Natalia could only give an inarticulate response.

'Come with me,' he said roughly. 'I'm crazy for you.'

'Clay—'

'We'll work things out.'

He was manipulating her with that caressing voice and the slow slide of his fingers across her skin, and the touch of his mouth at the corners of hers, and then under her ear. She flinched when he closed his teeth gently on the exquisitely sensitive lobe.

He whispered, 'Say yes, Natalia, sweet witch, come and live with me.'

'Yes,' she groaned as his tongue stabbed into the inner reach of her ear, and she went up in flames. Some day, she thought dazedly, some day she'd pay him back—somehow...

A cough splintered their heated, sensuous moment; Natalia stiffened, but Clay held her locked against him, looking above her head at the intruder.

'What is it?' he asked, his voice intimidating.

'I called in to see Natalia.'

Phil. A note of defiance in his voice, a resolution she'd never heard before. Clay's arms tightened, but when she looked up at him with angry eyes he let her go.

Turning, hoping that her face didn't show the effects of dazed passion, she said, 'Hello, Phil.'

He looked sick, white around the mouth, his eyes turbulent. 'I called in to see whether there was anything I could do for you.'

'No, there's nothing, thank you,' Natalia said, hating to hurt him, knowing she had to.

Phil looked from her face to Clay's and then back again. In his face she saw a kind of grey horror. He tried to speak a couple of times, then managed to say, 'Last night he said you were here when the—when someone cut down the capsicums.'

A small frown pleated her brows. 'Yes—I was asleep,' she said quietly.

He wet his lips. 'And you only went with him—with Clay—when—after you found them. The capsicums.'

'Yes.'

He stared at her. 'I came in,' he said. 'When I came home after dropping Rachel off I saw the lights at the homestead and I turned around and came down here. I knocked on the door but no one answered.'

Natalia stiffened, and Clay's hand gripped her shoulder, giving her support. 'I was tired,' she said. 'I've been getting up every two hours during the last two nights to check the hydroponics. One of the steers broke a valve.'

Keeping his eyes on the ground, Phil nodded. 'I thought you were at the homestead with him, and I—' he wet his lips '—and I think I must have had a brainstorm. I went over to the tunnel-house and saw that someone had stolen the computer and I—I cut all the plants.'

Natalia's head spun. Clay's other hand came up to hold her upright, but after a moment she stiffened her shoulders and looked fully at the man she had always liked, always admired for his steadfast devotion to duty. 'Why?' she asked clearly.

He said with a hopeless attempt at a smile, 'I was jealous. So it serves me right that what—what I did drove you to spend the night with him. Natalia, I'm very sorry. I must have been mad, but I won't ever bother you again. And I—I wish you all the best.'

He gave a jerky nod and blundered around the side of the house.

Clay's hand tightened on her shoulders, 'Where do you think you're going?'

Natalia listened to Phil's vehicle start up and go too fast down the drive, then said wretchedly, 'I wish I hadn't ever gone out with him. I didn't mean to hurt him.'

'The poor fool was obsessed with you,' Clay said harshly. 'However, I think he's realised how dangerous that obsession was.' He turned her and looked at her, golden eyes piercing and ruthless. 'You can't do anything for him beyond keeping away from him.'

'You knew,' she said wonderingly. 'How did you know it was Phil?'

He paused, then pulled her into his arms. 'The way he behaved last night, I think. Also, the cattle and the computer and the fencing materials had been professional jobs, done with quick, tidy precision. Whoever had slashed the capsicums had been savagely angry. The two didn't go together.'

Natalia shivered. 'I thought I knew him,' she said quietly, drawing strength from Clay's solid warmth and strength.

'It's always a shock to be faced with a friend's perfidy.' He kissed her forehead. 'You need a change of air. Pack what you want to take and we'll go to Auckland.'

Natalia felt her mouth drop. 'Just like that? Clay, I can't leave—'

'What's keeping you here?'

Bulldozed by the driving force of his will, she said, 'The hens—'

'Mrs Kaiwhare will be up this afternoon to pick them up.'

'The Ogilvies—'

'Will be just as happy to deal with you in Auckland through fax and phone.' He was relentless.

'But the homestead—'

His eyes kindled. 'I only stayed because of you.'

He was right—Xanadu had never been her dream. Now, faced with the ruin of everything she'd worked for, and Phil's pain, and—yes, why not admit it?—the gossip that her moving in with Clay would cause, she was racked by an urgency, a cowardly desire to get out of Bowden and leave behind the wreckage of her father's fantasies.

Torn by indecision, she pulled herself free of his arms and stared down at the peeling paint on the balustrade. 'I'll be running away.'

'From what? There's nothing here for you now. Come with me.' His voice was hard, almost merciless.

Natalia glanced at him, hoping for something—some tenderness—in the handsome, autocratic face.

He was watching her with such stark hunger, such consuming, compelling need, that her throat and mouth dried and her pulses began to thunder. Surely, she thought desperately, his desire and passion must eventually lead to the love she craved?

If she didn't take this chance of happiness, she didn't deserve it.

'Yes,' she said, flooded with the ironic peace of surrender when he smiled at her.

CHAPTER NINE

CLAY'S Auckland home was in a development of town-houses halfway up one of the green cones that dotted the isthmus. Superbly designed, to make the most of the sun and the spell-binding views, the houses had been set in gardens that paid tribute to Mediterranean shores and to New Zealand's magnificent heritage of rainforest trees and shrubs. Natalia looked gravely around.

'This is lovely,' she said quietly.

Flowers bloomed in a garden courtyard bordered by a high, close-clipped hedge. Beyond it rose the grassy slopes of the little extinct volcano, topped by a cluster of ancient puriri trees, their huge limbs bowed to the ground.

'Thank you,' Clay said.

She looked at him sharply. 'Did you design it?'

'No.' Smiling, he put down the two cases they'd brought to open the front door. 'It's the only urban development I've been involved in,' he said, picking her up and walking into the wide, tiled hallway. 'I wanted something that suited the site, and because no one seemed able to understand my vision, I found an architect and landscaper who did.' He looked down at her with a smile tilting his mouth and a deep, intense warmth in his gaze.

'Welcome home,' he said as he shouldered a door open, and kissed her and put her down, watching as she gazed around his sitting room.

A certain severity marked the room, although the over-stuffed furniture was skilfully matched and contrasted. Books filled a large set of shelves, and the pictures were varied and interesting. The room radiated the fresh, light beauty of winter flowers—tulips and jonquils and the heavenly blue of irises—which indicated a housekeeper with her own key.

It suited Clay. Natalia had expected a starkly modern apartment with even more stark furniture; she found this infinitely more pleasant. Not that it mattered, because she had no right to object. In spite of his irritation at the term, and his attempt to make her feel better about it, she was now Clay's mistress, bought and paid for. Before they had left Bowden they'd visited the solicitor, and Clay had organised the disposal of her property and the payment of her debt.

'What's the matter?' he asked abruptly.

Meeting narrowed eyes in an expressionless face, she said, 'I've just realised what burning your boats means, I suppose.'

'Regrets, Natalia?' When he touched her shoulder she had to stop herself from swaying towards him as naturally and inevitably as a coconut palm greets the tropical lagoon. She couldn't afford the luxury of dependence.

'A few,' she admitted.

His lashes half covered his eyes, giving him a distinctly saturnine cast. Beneath them, intent and golden, his eyes gleamed. 'Come and see the bedroom,' he suggested.

Her smile wavered slightly, was repinned firmly to her mouth. Why feel so defeated? Clay had made no bones about the reason he wanted her with him. And although she loved him, she had to accept that he might never progress beyond this violent passion.

I could end up with a broken heart, she thought, walking beside him down a wide hall. Well, when it happens I'll deal with it.

This was an honest relationship; Clay hadn't lied to her.

For the bedroom the decorator had chosen a subtle mixture of gold and amber and tan, anchored by small areas of black. The large bed wore a cover tailored in stripes of black and cinnamon-brown that matched the padded bedhead. Two armchairs upholstered in an unusual cinnamon and ivory check sat on either side of a table in the window; the pictures were an interesting mix of modern and traditional styles.

'No people,' Natalia said.

He followed her gaze. 'No,' he said on a surprised note. 'I hadn't realised until you said that, but I've never liked figures in a landscape.'

'I'd never have thought you'd like abstracts. Is that a Georgette Edwards?' Natalia nodded at one subtle, clever oil, black and bronze and copper dominated by a brilliant, heart-shaking blue.

'Yes. Do you know her?'

'I know her work. It's fabulous.' And expensive, and usually an acquired taste; Clay had said he knew little about art, but if he liked Georgette Edwards he had a connoisseur's eye.

'You're nervous,' Clay said, smiling his twisted smile.

She ran her forefinger along the polished wood of the dressing table. 'Yes. Silly, isn't it?'

'I think it's endearing,' he said, and came to stand behind her.

Slowly Natalia raised her head, looking at their reflections in the mirror. Against Clay's wide shoulders she seemed small and slender and fragile. Lazy golden eyes roamed her mirrored face with more than a hint of possessiveness as his long fingers closed around her upper arms.

'I think we should redecorate this room,' he said, a smile quirking his mouth.

'Why? It's a very nice room,' she protested, even as her heart leapt at the words he'd used—*we* should redecorate.

'It doesn't do you justice,' he said deliberately. 'It's too restrained, too calm. You should sleep in something that echoes your inherent drama—black and green and ivory, with the red of your mouth and the silky strength of your character.'

Heat sparked along her cheeks. What exactly did he mean by 'inherent drama'? Did he see her as anarchic and disorderly? 'No, this suits you,' she said, warming because he was intimating a shared future. 'Lovely tawny colours, like some great lion—a very leashed lion.'

He laughed. 'Perhaps the two of us could do with a bit of loosening up. You're too controlled—that lush mouth is under such constant restraint it's a wonder you haven't developed lines around it. Yet I'll bet you were a wild, temperamental little girl.'

Imprisoned by his hands, now sliding up and down her arms in a touch as gentle as it was exciting, Natalia stood very still, watching their mirror images. 'I had tantrums,' she agreed, noting the deepening colour in her skin, the glitter his lazy caress summoned in her heavy-lidded eyes. Her mouth was fuller and her breasts tightened, yearning for his touch.

Her breath caught in her throat. Twenty-four hours ago she'd been an independent human being; now she was in thrall to Clay's male sorcery. After years of carefully planning every move, she'd tossed everything aside to elope with a man who offered her a potent, primeval passion— but only a chance of permanence.

She'd never realised before that she was a gambler.

He bent his black head and kissed the acutely sensitive spot beneath her ear. 'Natalia,' he murmured. 'Make love to me, Natalia.'

Reaching up, her fingers searched through his thick, springy hair to shape the bones beneath. 'Yes,' she whispered.

'I like this room,' she said a long time later. 'You weren't serious about redecorating, were you?'

Clay tucked her head under his chin. 'I still have these fantasies about making love to you in a great, oriental bed with silks and brocades and furs,' he said meditatively.

She laughed with sleepy amusement. 'I'm all for indulging fantasies, but furs are no longer politically correct and it might be difficult to find comfortable brocades. I like this.'

'So do I,' he said, gliding a slow, sensuous hand from her waist to her hip.

His open, self-assured enjoyment of her body was almost shocking, yet she enjoyed the freedom it gave her to explore him in return. Touching the centre of his chest with the tip of her tongue, she asked, 'Do you have an office somewhere?'

'At the moment I work from home and use office temps when I need them,' he said indolently. 'How would you like to come to Hawke's Bay with me at the end of the week?'

'Do you want me to?'

He kissed the top of her head. 'I wouldn't ask if I didn't.'

'What will we be doing?'

'I'm checking out a run-down vineyard that makes some of the best wine in the world but needs a lot of money to expand. While we're there we could go to a jazz concert, or look at the gannets on Cape Kidnappers—whatever you want. Napier's a charming little city, full of Art Deco buildings.'

Mentally scrabbling through the contents of her suitcase, she said, 'I'd like that, but—'

'Good. We'd better buy you some clothes tomorrow.'

Natalia froze. When the silence had stretched beyond comfort level, he said evenly, 'I hope you're not going to be rigid and difficult about this.'

'I didn't think of clothes,' she muttered. 'I didn't realise you were going to take me with you when you went away.'

'The days are long gone when men hid their mistresses,' he said casually, although she heard the bite in the words. 'I'm not ashamed of you, Natalia, and I forbid you to be ashamed of yourself.' He turned her head and kissed her throat, biting softly down the pale length of it. With his mouth covering the fluttering hollow at the base, he murmured, 'I want to give you clothes that pay tribute to your beauty.' When he lifted his head, her heart jumped at the turbulence in the depths of his eyes.

'I'm sorry I ranted on about buying and selling; I know

this—us—our arrangement—isn't like that,' she said, because she was being ungracious. 'We'll buy some clothes, and whenever I put them on I'll think of you.'

Smiling, he made a necklace of kisses for her. 'Good,' he said, not trying to hide his satisfaction.

The following day Clay told the owner of a discreet salon, 'Not fashion. She's not fashionable. What she has is style.'

'I'll say,' the middle-aged, frighteningly well-groomed proprietor said, looking Natalia over with an impersonal eye. 'Right, style it is.'

Ten minutes later Natalia stared at herself in the mirror and wondered how often Clay had bought clothes for a woman.

None of your business, she told herself, twisting to see how the jacket fitted across her shoulders. As well as being easy to wear, the narrow trousers and exquisitely cut jacket made her look smart and confident and worldly—all the things she so conspicuously wasn't.

'Superb,' the proprietor said firmly, swishing back the curtain. 'You're built like a racehorse, all line and muscle. Do me a favour, will you? Never wear anything but black and red. Use that soft, pale ivory as a neutral, and green— the exact green of your eyes—when you're feeling adventurous.'

Natalia looked past her to Clay, lounging on a deep sofa. He lifted his brows and she emerged from the cubicle, feeling oddly, absurdly shy. And embarrassed. He'd asked if she wanted him to come with her and she'd said yes, but now she felt as though the salon owner—and everyone who'd seen them walk in together—knew that he was buying her clothes.

Buying her? The nasty little thought was banished. No, she had to believe that there was more to their relationship than buying and selling.

Getting to his feet, Clay looked her over, the austere

framework of his face giving nothing away. 'That suits you. I'm beginning to think the burglary was a good thing.'

'Suits her?' The older woman snorted. 'She wears clothes like a dream and you say they suit her! So you've had a burglary. It happens, it happens, and you can replace clothes. What else do you need, my dear?'

'Something to wear to dinner,' Natalia told her, trying to wrest back some control. Without actually lying Clay had saved her face, and for that she was grateful.

And alarmed, because he read her too easily.

She ended up with two pairs of trousers, a skirt, several variations on tops, and one jacket. For dinner she chose a dress in unrelieved black that could be worn during the day with the addition of the jacket.

'Good thinking. Those are classical styles, and you can dress the evening clothes up with diamonds,' the owner approved as she packed the clothes carefully. No one seemed to take down the prices, and certainly no money changed hands.

Did Clay do this sort of thing often? Natalia couldn't remember ever feeling jealous, but she burned with it now.

'Can I make a suggestion?' the older woman said without missing a beat. 'Have your hair cut and styled. You look as though you've been hacking at it with the kitchen scissors.'

'I have.' Natalia was unrepentant.

Half-appalled, half-laughing, the woman exchanged a complicated glance with Clay. 'Go to Steffan's,' she advised. 'He's a pain in the neck but he's a genius with scissors. Make sure he doesn't do anything outrageous. And get his make-up assistant to show you what cosmetics to use. I'll ring him if you like—he and I have an arrangement. I'm his mother.'

Natalia never knew whether it was a feminine need to look her best, or—embarrassingly—a jealous desire to measure up to the other women who'd shared Clay's bed that stopped her instinctive objection.

Abandoning the question as unprofitable, she went

meekly off to the salon, and by the end of the day possessed not only a small, expensive pack of cosmetics and skin-care products, but a tamed head of hair, miraculously lighter and sleeker in spite of her curls. The new cut emphasised her eyes and lent her cheekbones more prominence.

'I wonder how he did that,' she said, staring at herself in the mirror in the big bedroom.

Clay laughed. 'Clearly he's a genius, as his mother said. One thing he couldn't do, however, is change that decisive chin and jaw.'

He lay sprawled on the bed, all long golden limbs and indolence—an indolence only skin-deep. Natalia gave her reflection a final doubtful glance before turning to him. 'You make me sound like a battleaxe.'

'You look what you are, a strong, incredibly desirable woman,' he said coolly.

She was wearing a slim, skin-coloured camisole and French knickers; they'd arrived by courier with the clothes and a note from the owner of the shop suggesting she go to a certain lingerie shop to be fitted for bras.

Heat stirred in Natalia again as Clay's eyes lingered on her breasts.

Unexpectedly he said, 'I enjoyed being with you when you bought those clothes today, and I can't think of anything I'd prefer than to be lying on this bed watching you as you are now.' His voice altered. 'Well, a few things. But it's not just the sex—I like being with you. I want you to be happy.'

'I want you to be happy too,' she said quietly. She might hunger for a more formal commitment, one that lasted for ever, but his pleasure in her was enough for now.

'I've got something else you might use,' he said after a moment, his voice neutral. He got up, sleek and lean and graceful, padded into the walk-in wardrobe that had been fitted beside an *en suite* bathroom, and returned with a brown paper parcel in one hand.

Natalia eyed it with bewilderment.

'It's not a snake,' he said coolly, handing it over.

No, it was a pad of drawing paper, with pencils—the correct ones. He'd got advice, because there was a craft knife there too. Natalia smoothed her hand over the pad. She had to swallow to ask huskily, 'Thank you. Why?'

'Because you have talent,' he said calmly. 'And because you're used to making every hour count. If you don't have something to do you'll go crazy. And I doubt if dedicated shopping would satisfy you. Which reminds me—I'll take you in tomorrow and we can set up a bank account and an allowance.'

Her throat closed. 'I could keep house,' she said gruffly.

'That would be just as much a waste of your talent as growing capsicums was. Besides, I have a housekeeper.' He spoke pleasantly, without too much interest—making conversation. Yet she thought she discerned a deliberate note in his words, as though he was working out a plan of attack.

'Thank you,' she said belatedly. 'I—I'm touched.' He'd insisted on bringing the sketches on the walls of the house at Xanadu, but she hadn't asked where he'd put them.

How had he known that the only way for her to deal with her compulsion to draw was to repress it? A shiver ran the length of her spine. She would have to be careful—he was far too astute.

And so easy to love.

A month later she stood in front of the mirror in the bathroom, applying cosmetics with a skilful hand. Clay had just rung from the car to tell her he'd be home soon; tonight they were going to a cocktail party given by one of the producer boards for the managing director of a huge British textile firm.

Natalia blotted her scarlet lips and stared gravely at herself in the mirror. She'd hoped for intimacy, and she had it—but it was a strictly limited closeness. Clay made room for her in his life; he was proud of her, and his eyes smouldered whenever he saw her. But she knew little more of him after a month than she had when she'd arrived here. She was happy, of course she was. Clay was the perfect lover—intelligent, thoughtful, sexy, a man who worshipped her body with such skill, such flair and expertise, that her bones liquefied whenever she saw him. What woman wouldn't be happy?

A woman who loved him.

Coming to this lovely apartment, learning to love its owner, was the most dangerous thing she'd ever done. Scrutinising her face with its sleek, imperceptible mask of cosmetics, she wondered whether her gamble was paying off. Their month together had taught her the difference between an overmastering physical passion and love.

It had also taught her that she needed more from him than sexual adoration and friendship; if he couldn't love her she'd have to leave before she embarrassed him with demands he couldn't meet.

She heard the door and turned, summoning a smile. Her heart clamped as he came in, the excellent tailoring of his dark suit failing to hide the raw male power that emanated from him. 'Good day?' He'd spent it with the trade delegation.

'Pretty good.' His eyes kindled as they came to rest on her. 'I wish we didn't have to go out again tonight.'

'Me too,' she teased, hiding her fleeting wistfulness behind a smile.

He came over and kissed the back of her neck. 'I'll shower and change as fast as I can. With any luck we might be able to get away from this quickly.'

It was unlikely. If she'd learned anything this past month it was that Clay was seen as a coming man; leaders of the industry he'd chosen to make his career in respected him and wanted slices of him.

'I'd like that,' she said, reaching up to touch his cheek.

'I saw something else I thought you might like,' he said, dropping a small parcel on the marble counter.

Frowning, she looked at it.

'Open it,' Clay commanded with a tilted smile.

He bought her small things all the time—a golden lion charm dropped on her pillow a few days after she'd told him that his eyes reminded her of a lion's, a book she'd wanted to read, an antique feather boa the exact colour of her eyes, a print she'd admired—but he'd never bought her jewellery before. Her fingers trembled as she undid the paper and opened the box. Hope flared—and died as she saw earrings, each a glittering green stone surrounded by diamonds.

'Yes, they match your eyes,' Clay said, picking out one of the beautiful things to hold against her face. His smile narrowed. 'Exactly.'

Natalia bit her lip. Words tumbled to her mouth, were discarded. At last she said, 'Clay, I can't accept these.'

'Why not?'

'I didn't—I wasn't expecting anything...'

'I know.' Some secret emotion glimmered in his eyes. 'It pleases me to give you things. Don't be so prickly, darling. Earrings, however expensive, are not a chain of ownership. They don't compromise that liberty you value so highly.'

She could only accept such extravagance if it was given with love. Rallying, she said, 'You think that whenever you lower your voice an octave I'm putty in your hands, don't you?'

'Mmm,' he said, kissing first one earlobe and then the other. 'Wear them for me, Natalia.'

She'd wear them because they gave him pleasure. If she had to go she'd leave them behind. 'I haven't got anything for you,' she said foolishly.

Clay laughed, a smokily sensual sound. 'You're the only gift I want,' he said, straightening up. 'I'd better get ready.'

While he showered she put on the dress Liz had given her and slid the loops of the earrings through the lobes of her ears, looking at her reflection with troubled eyes. In spite of the care Clay had taken to match her eyes, jewellery was oddly impersonal, whereas the book he'd bought her had been chosen with her taste in mind.

So had these, she tried hard to convince herself.

And he'd certainly understood her needs when he'd bought the sketching pad and the pencils; she'd flung herself into her forgotten hobby with the vehemence of long deprivation, sketching wherever they went.

Although she hadn't tried to capture Clay on paper.

Tomorrow, she decided, setting her lips firmly. Tomorrow she'd stop drifting in this sensuous haze and get on with her life. She'd make plans, search out something to do, a career—at twenty-three she was still young enough to train, even to change her mind if she wanted to.

The room in one of the city's most luxurious hotels was opulently furnished and decorated, with huge arrangements of flowers—tulips from the South Island and white scented lilies, probably from tunnel-houses, Natalia decided with an ironic little smile. They looked stunning.

So did the guests. Most of the men were in dinner jackets or severe dark suits. Aware that she was one of the few women not dressed in black, Natalia was even more conscious of the weight of the emeralds and diamonds in her ears. And if she had been able to ignore them, enviously appreciative glances would have reminded her.

Clay was at her side, his hand resting lightly on the small of her back. Was he being more possessive than usual? Did it have anything to do with the earrings?

Stop it, she ordered. You're overreacting, and it's stupid.

They were talking to a small group of people, mostly men, mostly sheep farmers from the South Island high country whose main export was exquisitely fine merino wool. A flash of colour caught her eye—a soft, very pretty pink dramatised by a hint of silver—worn by a young woman heading towards them. With an involuntary smile on her lips, Natalia looked at the other brave, unfashionable soul.

The woman didn't respond; her eyes were fixed on Clay's face.

Then Clay suddenly saw her—and froze.

Fiercely, swiftly, Natalia glanced at the woman from beneath her lashes. Not beautiful, although she had stunning blue eyes and lovely skin. A generous, quivering mouth, a good figure, and money; that dress hadn't been cheap.

Urbanely Clay broke off his conversation and looked down at Natalia. 'Can I get you a drink?' he asked.

Natalia knew she should say yes, knew she should give him the chance to speak to this woman by himself. Her mouth hardened as she fought an ignoble, selfish jealousy. 'No, thank you,' she said, despising herself for yielding to it.

Humiliation swept over her, because of course he knew. Her spine stiffened; she met his level glance with hidden defiance.

Clay turned. 'Hello, Tess,' he said easily. 'I didn't expect to see you here.'

Relief was mirrored in blue eyes, trembled in her smile. 'Clay,' she said in a light, clipped voice, 'how lovely to see you. I was beginning to think I didn't know a soul in the room except for Dad and Steve.'

'Tess, this is Natalia Gerner,' Clay said. 'Natalia, meet Tess Jamieson.'

'Tess Farrier,' the woman said rapidly, giving Natalia a swift, friendly smile before turning back to Clay. 'When I left Dean I went back to my own name. Quite frankly, the less I'm reminded of the Jamiesons the happier I'll be—just like you!'

Dean Jamieson's ex-wife was older than she looked—late twenties, Natalia decided, concentrating on that because it was better to fix on unimportant details. If she'd let Clay go off to get her drink she might not have ever known who the woman in the pink dress was. No doubt it served her right.

At least Tess didn't seem to realise who Natalia was. Of course, she probably didn't know—after all, Dean wouldn't have told his wife that he'd been trying to bed his neighbour in Northland.

And what did she mean by that last comment?

'Clay, is it true that you bought Pukekahu?' Tess went on eagerly.

'Yes.'

Tess Farrier laughed bitterly. 'I'll bet Dean didn't know you were the buyer! If I hadn't left him he'd have held on to Pukekahu and let it rot into the ground just to spite you. So you can thank me for finally getting you the place—he had to sell because my father insisted on hiring a horrendously expensive Auckland lawyer, and he's sticking Dean for all he's worth. Pukekahu wasn't in the Jamieson Family Trust, so it was the obvious one to go.'

'You realise he's here?' Clay asked quietly.

'Of course I know he's here! That's the object of the exercise—to show him I'm not weeping at home on my own.' Tess gave Natalia a sudden, rueful smile. 'I'm sorry,' she said, 'I've been very rude, but—well, when my ex-husband was tom-catting all around New Zealand, Clay was the only one who understood how I felt. He hates his stepbrother too—though not as much as Dean hates him.'

Thank God for the mask of her cosmetics. Thank God for Clay's hand on her arm—for a horrible moment it was the only reason she stayed on her feet. Natalia nodded, pretending that she'd known, pretending that everything was all right. She tried very hard to relax the tense muscles in her jaw and shoulders, but Tess Farrier's blinding smile knotted them again.

'Oh, there's Dad,' Tess said, waving. 'I'd better go. Great to see you, Clay, and to meet you, Natalia. I'm surprised I haven't seen Dean—I know he's here.' She gave another smile, this one jaded and cynical. 'Flattering all the delegation wives and trying to cut himself a special deal, so Dad says. Bye.'

She bestowed a real smile on Clay, then switched it to Natalia; it lost something in the translation. Still smiling, she headed towards a solid man with the lined brown face of a farmer, who nodded at Clay across the intervening people.

Blindly, Natalia stared around the room. She couldn't think, and blessedly couldn't feel.

'We'll go home,' Clay said, his hand supporting her, his voice cool and objective, as though being found out in lie after lie didn't worry him at all.

Nauseated, she went with him, but the evening wasn't over yet. As they went through the doors and out into the foyer a figure detached itself from a group, and Dean Jamieson's voice fell like a clap of doom.

'Nat!' he exclaimed. 'What—?'

Clay's hand gripped her arm so fiercely that she almost cried out in pain; it relaxed immediately, but he didn't let her go.

'Hello, Dean,' she said, her voice echoing thinly in her ears.

He took a step towards them, his handsome face incredulous, his eyes flicking from Natalia's face to Clay's and then back again. Amazingly he turned the swift drop of his jaw into a slow, sneering smile. 'Well, little stepbrother,' he taunted, 'still eating my leavings?'

Natalia froze, appalled at both the lie and his open provocation.

In a controlled, dangerous voice Clay said, 'Dining off acorns yet, Dean? It won't be long. You're not the man your father was, and I hear that Jamieson Pastoral was hard hit by the drought. You should have spent some money on Pukekahu when you owned it—the North had plenty of rain.'

He didn't seem to exert any pressure on Natalia, but they were past Dean before he was able to come up with a rejoinder beyond an ugly flush.

In the car Natalia recalled the reference—the prodigal son in the parable who'd wasted his inheritance and been reduced to caring for the swine and sharing their acorns. She looked down at her hands, still in her lap.

Traffic swished past, lights flaring through the soft drizzle, white and yellow and scarlet, reflecting in a dazzling shimmer off the wet road. Beside her Clay drove without speaking, his dark clothes absorbing light.

Silence weighed her shoulders, blocked her throat. No emotions, she told herself; you can't afford the luxury of emotions yet.

But in Clay's house she turned to him, her eyes glittering, and asked passionately, 'What the hell is going on? Why didn't you tell me that Dean Jamieson is your stepbrother?'

Dropping the car keys on to the hall table, he said deliberately, 'I told you I was adopted—Olivia Freeman was my adoptive mother. She was Jamieson's second wife—his first marriage produced Dean. I presume Olivia couldn't have children. Whatever, Dean hated both Olivia and the brat she brought into the family.'

Rage was far simpler to deal with than the pain of betrayal so she let it roar through her, cutting away any prospect of common sense. In a voice so cold it should have frozen him right through to his bones she said, 'Then why are you Clay Beauchamp, not Clay Jamieson?'

He came across and took her hands in his. 'You're cold,' he said, frowning.

She jerked them away, clenching them into fists because more than anything else she wanted to leave them in his warm grip. *'What is this all about?'*

'The name change is quite simple. When Olivia died I decided that I no longer wanted to be called Jamieson. I went back to my birth mother's name.' He spoke with an infuriating patience. 'Pukekahu was Olivia's childhood home.'

Natalia pressed her lips together to hold back the cry of feral pain. 'I'd already worked that out. Why didn't you tell me?'

'I didn't want anyone to know.' His eyes narrowed in a granite face. 'Tess was right—he'd have burnt the station to the ground and sown it in salt rather than let me buy it.'

'But afterwards? After you'd bought it? Why didn't you tell me then?'

He said with sudden violence, 'Because I loathe him—and it was fairly common knowledge that you'd had an affair with him. I was so jealous I couldn't bear the thought of it, so I pushed it to the back of my mind. I didn't want him spoiling what we have.'

Natalia drew in a deep, shuddering breath. Control, she reminded herself—keep your temper under control. Very quietly, very firmly, she told him, 'I did not have an affair with him.' Heat crawled across her skin. 'I know I made love with you when I scarcely knew you, but I don't make a habit of it. Yes, I found Dean attractive, and we went out together for a while, but I didn't sleep with him, if that's what's causing you so much angst. When I found out that he was married—something he'd neglected to tell anyone in Bowden—I sent him on his way.'

'I see.'

His level tone told her nothing, but the hair on the back of her neck lifted. She looked up into eyes as enigmatic and unreadable as those of a wild animal, guarded, almost pitiless.

An image of masks floated in the front of her brain—masks that hid so much, altered faces she'd known all her life into mysterious strangers. Clay had kept his secrets well.

He was watching her with half-closed eyes, his expression unyielding. 'If we're discussing things kept hidden, why did you tell me you barely knew him?'

CHAPTER TEN

'I DIDN'T know him at all,' Natalia said, colour burning along her cheekbones, her voice crisp and clear. 'I thought he was an attractive, interesting, charming man. When I found out that he was a louse I felt like a complete and utter idiot for being taken in.'

'It sounds as though you knew him very well.' Clay's voice was coolly neutral, his eyes guarded and watchful.

'I didn't have an affair with Dean,' she reiterated between her teeth. 'Yes, I was stupid enough to be interested in him, but I don't sleep with everyone I'm interested in. And I despise liars. Especially those who lie by omission.' Her tone was scathing.

When Clay didn't answer she went on incredulously, 'What made you think that your brother and I were lovers?'

'He's no brother of mine,' he said curtly. 'As for the other—'

'It was a stupid question,' she interrupted, hands clenching at her side. 'No doubt the good people of Bowden told you all about the non-existent affair! That was Dean getting his own back—as well as trashing my reputation he told everyone who'd listen that I'd known all along that he was married.'

She had seen Clay's eyes wary and cool and dispassionate, molten and tender and lazily sensuous, but she had never seen them as cold and hard as yellow quartz. 'But you didn't,' he said without expression.

Natalia's head came up. 'No,' she said quietly. Did he believe her? It was impossible to tell.

'You'd made love before.'

The colour leached from her face, pointing up the fragile

153

bones. 'When I was eighteen—twice. We thought we were in love, and we'd planned to get married after we'd finished university. Then my mother died and I knew I wasn't ever going to get away from Xanadu, so making love with him was a kind of farewell.'

She had to stop, to drag in a breath, to listen to the lurching beat of her heart.

Ask him, she told herself. Ask him.

How did you ask your lover whether he'd wooed you and made love to you, persuaded you into a relationship as revenge on a man he hated? No, she thought, that was sheer melodrama—Clay wasn't so twisted that he'd do that.

But the thought niggled, like poison in honey; she could still hear the note of scathing disdain in Clay's words when he spoke of Dean.

'I see.' Clay's voice was still non-committal. 'I shouldn't have asked—it doesn't matter.'

'Did you—?' She stopped. She couldn't ask; Clay wouldn't say, Well, yes, as it happens, it did occur to me that one way I could really drive my stepbrother crazy was to take as a mistress the woman who wouldn't sleep with him, so I set out to do that.

No, she wasn't thinking straight. He thought she'd been Dean's lover.

He asked, 'Did I what?'

Quickly she substituted, 'Why didn't you tell me you believed I'd had an affair with Dean?'

His mouth hardened. 'I found it distasteful that you should have fallen prey to his shoddy, meretricious appeal.' He watched her with hooded eyes, his well-cut evening clothes turning him into an intimate stranger. 'And I was bitterly jealous—as jealous and resentful as poor bloody Phil. I didn't want you feeling sorry for me, as you felt sorry for him. Why does it matter so much? It's made no difference—you're here with me.'

'Yes,' she said numbly, relinquishing hope.

Clay wanted her, he enjoyed making love to her—he even

lost himself in the carnal pleasures of her body—but he didn't want any sort of commitment. She had given herself entirely to a man who saw her as a lover, not a wife.

Yet for her the passion and enjoyment they found in each other was no longer enough. If she couldn't have everything, she'd rather have nothing. Eating acorns was not her style— she'd rather die, she thought passionately, than have Clay feel sorry for her. Her hand clenched at her side; the green silk glinted as the skirt clung to her skin and then sighed free. Odd that she should have been wearing Liz's gorgeous silk dress the night she met Clay and now, the night she realised it was all over.

Somewhere she'd read something about hope—'Hope deferred maketh the heart sick.' She could quote from the Bible too, she thought painfully.

And hope deferred died. She knew that now. Hers was bitter ashes in her mouth when she said, 'You should have told me.'

'Perhaps we should have told each other. Is Dean the reason you asked if I was married?'

'I wasn't going to make that mistake again.'

'If you'd asked Dean he'd have lied.' Clay's calm, judicial tone was chilling.

'I know,' she said, turning away. 'He didn't feel the existence of a wife should stop us becoming lovers. It took me some time to convince him that I thought otherwise.'

'I don't imagine he liked that.'

'No.' She hesitated, then gave a tiny shrug. 'There was a nasty scene. I hadn't realised he thought I was up for sale. He couldn't see any problem—to him it was entirely straightforward. I'd sleep with him whenever he wanted me to, and in return he'd pay my debts.'

'Money is his only measure.' Anger flashed a moment in Clay's eyes, but his expression didn't alter.

So now he knew why she'd responded so violently to his suggestion that they live together. 'I noticed,' she said quietly. 'He didn't dent my heart, Clay—just my pride a bit.'

And her confidence in her judgement. A thought struck her. 'And Phil—did you think I'd had an affair with him too?'

Frowning, he answered, 'You told me you didn't—of course I believed you.'

'Do you believe now that I didn't sleep with Dean?' She didn't know why she was pushing.

'Of course I do,' he repeated evenly, his lips thinning in impatience. 'Why should you lie? Your emotional life before we met has nothing to do with me.'

Because the only thing that interested him was her presence in his bed. While she'd been falling further and further in love with him, he hadn't changed at all.

That was when Natalia knew that her time had run out; she had to leave him before loving him shattered her life into pieces so small she'd never be able to reassemble it.

She'd go tomorrow, she thought, letting anger drive the pain underground, but before she went she'd give him something he'd never forget. If ever he married he'd remember tonight as he said his vows, and however much he loved his wife, Natalia would haunt him.

As he'd haunt her.

She needed to know something else. 'Why didn't you tell me that you and he were stepbrothers?'

'I didn't want Dean to suspect that I was behind the offer for Pukekahu. You know what small towns are like; somehow it would have got to him. And I'd been told that you and he had had some sort of relationship—for all I knew it still existed. By the time I was sure it was over, I just wanted to push the possibility of you being his lover out of my mind.'

Natalia nodded, asking, 'If Olivia was your adoptive mother, how did Dean get his hands on Pukekahu?'

'She left it to him.'

Her heart jerked. He hadn't moved, but she knew this had been the greatest betrayal of his life. 'Why?' she whispered.

'God knows,' he said, his eyes cold and implacable. 'She left me a reasonable inheritance in shares and bonds.'

'So Dean let the place run down because he knew it would hurt you.'

'I can think of no other reason,' he said indifferently.

Yes, she could imagine Dean Jamieson deliberately ruining a place because someone he disliked had loved it. How could she have been so stupid as to be fooled by his facile charm? 'Is that why you bought it? Because Olivia loved it?'

Clay's brows lifted. 'Sentiment has no place in business,' he said aloofly. 'It's a good investment property. I don't waste time or money or effort on spiting people.'

No, she thought with a shiver, you get even.

He came towards her. 'Natalia, forget it. It's not worth fretting over.'

'I know,' she said, turning to him, her lashes lowered and her mouth curved softly, lying to him, lying to herself. It was already too late; she'd never forget him. But for her sanity, her self-esteem, she had to leave him and make some sort of life for herself.

Tomorrow...

She reached up and linked her arms about his neck, feeling the familiar lurch of her heart, the unsteady thud of her pulses.

'All right?' he asked, his eyes narrowed and intent as he scanned her face.

'Of course,' she said in a smoky little voice, pulling his head down.

It was instantaneous, that combustion of the senses; she had only to touch him and he wanted her. And she, God help her, was as much a prisoner of desire's honeyed, fiery chains as he was.

Against his mouth she whispered, 'Are you going to make me wait?'

He laughed beneath his breath, a lazy sound sensuous as the purr of a big cat, and kissed her, his mouth teasing yet urgent, hinting at the potent power she could unleash in him.

Natalia's mouth opened under his, famished and desper-

ate. This was a perilous game; if she was to do this she had
to stay cool and in control, not lose her head.

A woman scorned, she thought savagely, needed all her
wits about her. Except that she wasn't scorned; Clay had
never lied. She had overstepped the boundaries of their
agreement, not him.

Deeply, Clay said, 'Don't you want dinner?'

'I have a better idea,' she murmured, tracing the full outline of his lower lip with the tormenting tip of her tongue.
She rejoiced at the sudden increase of his breathing rate, at
the dusky colour that licked across the arrogant cheekbones,
at the darkness swallowing up the gold in his eyes.

'I can see that.' His arms tightened across her back.

And the doorbell rang.

Clay swore beneath his breath; as though he'd heard,
Dean shouted from outside, 'Let me in, damn you!'

Slowly, like a stallion scenting a rival, Clay's head lifted.
He was still looking at Natalia, but passion had been replaced by the remorseless, impersonal patience of a preda-
tor—and a certain grim satisfaction, she thought, ice enclosing her heart.

'You—Clay Whatever-you-call-yourself—if you don't let
me in I'll break the door down!'

'He must be drunk.' Natalia spoke with distaste and a
flicker of fear.

'Possibly,' Clay said. 'Go into the bedroom. This is between him and me; it's nothing to do with you.'

'I'll stay,' she said.

He dropped a fierce, swift kiss on her mouth, then put
her behind him and opened the door.

Flushed, his handsome face distorted, Dean slammed inside. Clay kicked the door shut and, before Dean had fully
gained his balance, moved with swift, deadly speed to put
himself between the intruder and Natalia.

'You little bitch,' Dean snarled, his blue eyes filled with
gloating malice. 'God, I knew you were mercenary, but you
couldn't bloody wait, could you? I told you I'd set us up,

get rid of Tess—it's taken time because the bitch wants more than her share! I *told* you I'd do it. Why couldn't you have waited? I would have married you!' He cast a look of pure hatred at Clay. 'As for you, you swine, I'll make you sorry you ever poached—'

'You haven't got a knife now,' Clay said indifferently.

A knife? Natalia's heart jolted as she glimpsed the scar on his face. Had Dean done that with a knife?

Hard and lethal and completely without emotion, Clay went on, 'And if you want a fight, be prepared to lose.'

That calm, contemptuous voice stopped Dean as though he'd been slapped. Scarlet-faced, his jaw jutting arrogantly, he scoffed, 'I wouldn't dirty my hands with a whore's son. You're *nothing*—white trash, bad seed. In the end even Olivia saw through you—she thought so little of you she left the only thing she valued to me. You had to *buy* Pukekahu.'

Natalia sucked in a breath. Clay's mouth lifted in that twisted smile. 'I'm sure she had her reasons,' he said tonelessly.

Natalia had learned to love this man; she respected him for his rock-solid integrity, for his strength of mind and his determination, his control and initiative, but she'd never admired him so much as she did then.

Thwarted, Dean swung back to Natalia. 'You played your hand too soon,' he sneered, grinning, completely confident that Clay would believe his lies. 'You could have been my wife instead of this man's whore.'

She didn't look at Clay. 'I'd rather be his mistress than your wife.'

'Do you really think he's going to keep you now he knows we were lovers?' Dean taunted brutally. 'Ever since my stupid stepmother brought him home—a filthy, foul-mouthed little bastard with no breeding, no family—he's wanted what's mine. He's never been able to get it—and it's always going to eat into him that I had you first. He'll dump you.'

Natalia shrugged. 'I think he knows you well enough to recognise your lies when he hears them,' she said quietly.

He gave the man he hated a swift, measuring glance, then attacked again. 'But they're not lies. Does he know that you only shacked up with him for his money?'

There was a moment of silence. Dean burst out laughing. 'Ah, little *brother*, she got you there, didn't she? Poor sucker. I hope you think she's worth it!'

'Get out.' Clay's voice was low and furious.

Dean stared insolently at him. 'Make me. You can't, can you? You've never been able to, you yellow—'

Before Natalia had stifled her gasp, Clay had an armlock on the struggling, cursing Dean, flattening him so close against the wall that Dean had to whip his face sideways to be able to breathe.

Ignoring his stepbrother's furious curses, Clay commanded, 'Open the door, Natalia.'

Although Dean shouted and writhed, he couldn't escape Clay's grip. Natalia skirted them and pulled the door back against the wall. In one smooth, immensely powerful movement, Clay lifted Dean and hurled him through the doorway.

Seldom, Natalia thought vengefully, had she enjoyed anything so much as seeing Dean Jamieson skid on to the path outside and lie there for an astonished, humiliated moment with rain pelting down on him. All dignity fled, he scrambled to his feet.

'Come out and fight like a man,' he blustered, but with a fleeting air of nervousness that robbed his innuendoes of their poison.

'When I find a man to fight I might,' Clay said coolly.

Dean stood his ground, until Clay took a step towards him. Backing away, he shouted, 'Well, Natalia, when you get sick of this jerk give me a ring—I might be tempted, although I certainly won't pay for your services!'

He turned; Natalia realised that he was nowhere as confident as he wanted to seem. Indeed, he scrabbled for the gate and got himself through it with a speed that was both ludicrous and embarrassing.

As Clay shut the door she dragged in a deep breath and said, 'You had to live with that for how long?'

'Ten years, give or take a few months,' Clay said levelly.

'I'm sorry,' she said numbly.

'What for?'

She shuddered. 'Sorry that for a few weeks I found him interesting and entertaining. It left you open to that—that flood of malice and lies.' Wiping a shaking hand across her mouth, she said, 'He must be utterly stupid to think we'd believe him.'

Clay reached out and pulled her into his arms. The aggression he'd disciplined so ferociously hummed through him like an electric current, and as he lifted her she could feel it transmuting into sexual energy.

Kissing her throat, he said, 'His father always did. And I'm sorry that those ten years of hating me gave him the chance to score off me by tormenting you. I couldn't touch him because I'd have killed him.'

'You've got far more control than he has,' she said, linking her arms around his neck. 'Forget him—he's not worth wasting another moment over.'

'I've already wasted too much of my life on him,' he said harshly, and strode with her down the hall and into their bedroom.

Into *his* bedroom, because she'd never been more than a temporary guest. But after tonight, she thought fiercely, he'd never make love to another woman in this room without remembering Natalia Gerner.

She'd lay claim to him with passion and fire and a searing completeness that would imprint her on his memory until the day he died.

He went to put her down on the bed, but she said, 'No. I want to make love to you,' so he lowered her to the ground.

His eyes narrowed as he surveyed her. 'I thought you always did.'

'Humour me.'

She caught the reservation in his eyes, noted the momentary compression of his mouth, and thought, You don't like that, do you? Control is so important to you, and this time you won't be in control. This time is for me.

Carefully she removed his jacket and the black tie, kissing his tanned throat; carefully, her hands deliberate and caressing, she took out dress-studs, cufflinks, kissing the corded veins and sinews of his wrist, the palms of his hands, feeling with a potent pleasure his powerful muscles clench as her mouth clung to his skin.

When the white shirt was peeled away her breath caught. 'You are completely, wonderfully magnificent,' she whispered, sliding her hands up his arms, across his shoulders, then following the fine antique pattern of body hair down to his waist. His midriff contracted at her touch, and his face clamped into a watchful mask.

The sensual magic was working on her too, of course; already she could feel the delicious contrast between her tense muscles and the honeyed looseness hidden inside her, where her body was readying itself for him.

She sank to her knees and took off his shoes and socks, then rose and flicked his belt free and worked his trousers down, kissing the iron muscles of his thighs.

'That's enough,' he suddenly growled in a strained voice. Strong hands grabbed her shoulders, pulled her upright.

Natalia met the goaded, wary blaze of his eyes with a smile, then leaned forward to brush her heavy eyelashes over each nipple in turn.

His chest rose and fell on a sharp, harsh breath. 'Now it's my turn,' he said thickly.

But she shook her head. 'Not yet,' she murmured, and began to undress.

Dean was not the only man who'd called her a tease—it had happened with other frustrated men who hadn't been able to believe that she didn't want to make love with them. This time she deliberately adopted the persona, the mask.

Clay was too sophisticated to enjoy the obvious bump and grind routine, so she didn't even try. Instead she held his smouldering gaze with her own as she sinuously discarded her clothes, until she stood before him with nothing on but her thin silk briefs.

Arousal burned across the starkly prominent framework of his face. 'Are you trying to drive me crazy?' he asked in dangerously quiet tones.

'I certainly hope so.' Feline promise purred in each word.

He laughed deep in his throat. 'What next, then?'

'I think you should get into bed,' she said. A flicker of nervousness shivered through her, tarnishing for a second the heat of unsatisfied desire.

She banished it. She'd gone too far to turn back now.

Clay might never love her, but she loved him. Just this once she'd give him everything she could, use the erotic skills and knowledge she'd gained these past weeks to imprint herself on his life for ever.

With the male grace that was particularly his, he got into the bed, lean golden length stretched out across the white sheets, a dark lord waiting to be pleasured. Yet Natalia sensed the ambivalence in him.

No wonder! A childhood like his was almost guaranteed to turn him into a man who needed to retain authority. Tonight he was going to discover the joys of letting go, of being the one who received rather than gave.

'Lie on your front,' she said.

His brows shot up. 'On my front?'

Bending, she bit gently into the smooth swell of his shoulder, letting him feel the sharpness of her teeth, then kissing the small red mark. 'On your front,' she repeated.

'Will I ever get the chance to order you around?' he asked in a voice charged with lazy sensuality.

Her heart began to pump wildly. 'Perhaps.'

Laughing quietly, he turned and presented his back to her, his profile an autocratic silhouette against the pillow.

Such sheer masculine beauty brought an ache to her throat. Why hadn't she asked him to pose for her?

Well, she could commit his image to her memory, mentally draw the golden wedge of shoulders to hips, the clean male lines, the flexible indentation of his spine, the taut curves of his backside and the long, strong legs.

Dry-mouthed, determined, she knelt beside him, and with her fingertips began to touch him so lightly she could scarcely feel anything of his skin beyond the heat; she concentrated on lifting the unseen body hairs, floating the tips of her fingers across the sinews where his neck joined his body, over tanned skin smooth as glove leather, feeling invisible hairs lick the sensitive skin of her fingertips—and hoping that such a subtle caress had the same effect on him as it had on her.

'What the hell are you doing?' he demanded gutturally.

'Don't you like it?'

After a taut second he gave a muffled, mirthless laugh. 'Too much. Have you taken lessons in seduction?'

'Only from you,' she said in a low voice, moving that maddening massage to his shoulders. It was torment to her too—as she softened and grew hot inside she had to stop herself from pressing into the coil and flex and contraction of muscle.

Beneath her fingertips his skin shuddered, and sweat began to glisten in the light of the lamps.

Lovingly Natalia attended to those parts of him she'd discovered to be extra sensitive; she swept an invisible current of sexuality down his spine before lingering on the hollows of his back, delicately skating across the tight buttocks.

Aware only of the thudding of her heart, of the unfelt texture of his skin, of the heat and scent of aroused male, of his bespelled, reluctant acquiescence, she canvassed the inside of his thighs and his calves, rejoicing at the quivering pull of muscle beneath the skin, the tension that gripped him when she reached the soles of his feet.

'Roll over,' she said, surprised at the hoarse note in her voice. Of course her unhurried, loving exploration of his body, her claim-staking progress, had fired her too. Liquid need weakened her; when he rolled over shock at his rampant readiness clouded her brain.

The fierce command in his face—the stark hunger there—was its own reward, and she settled down to work her way down his front with her skimming, almost-caresses.

Immediately his heavy eyelids lowered so that all she could see through the thick lashes were slivers of incandescent gold. His hands suddenly knotted by his sides and he turned his head restlessly on the pillow.

'How much longer are you going to keep this up?' he demanded in a voice edged with desperation.

'Until I finish,' she said. How could that be her voice? Husky and weighted and slow, each word lagging...

Clay said roughly, 'Or I do.'

She bent and kissed his navel, slipping the tip of her tongue around the tight indentation, and progressed further down with the torturous provocation of fleeting touch after fleeting touch.

The cords in his neck stood out; flames licked the golden slits beneath his lashes. She heard his breath catch in his throat, and the long groan that erupted was music, all she had ever wanted to hear.

Through lips that barely moved he said, 'You'd better be ready.'

'Not yet,' she said, and began that leisurely, delicate torture again.

He said nothing, but she could feel the ferocious willpower that chained his instincts to obedience, and knew how much his mastery was costing him.

It was costing her too; her body was one violent, clamouring ache that screamed for satiation. At last relenting, she straddled him, but stayed poised on her knees, refusing to slide that last inch.

Eyes swallowed up in darkness, he asked through lips that barely moved, 'Proving a point, Natalia?'

'Perhaps.'

'Then move carefully if you want to get something out of this.'

The inexorable grip of hunger shivered through her every cell. 'I've already got what I want out of it,' she said huskily, easing herself down.

She expected him to grasp her hips, but although sweat beaded his forehead and glistened in the fine hair on his chest he didn't move, and she had to guide herself on to him.

Clay's chest lifted suddenly as, moving only her internal muscles, she lowered herself that last inch and began to pull him into her. In spite of a mouth that had tightened into a thin line and a jutting, angular jaw, the hands that fastened around her wrists were almost gentle.

Sensation raced from the fragile bones beneath his fingers to her innermost core. Green eyes locking with smouldering golden ones, neither conceding an advantage, she enclosed him until he was buried to the hilt.

Dazed by an unbidden rapture, she froze, but after a few moments summoned enough energy to begin to rock, riding his loins with her own considerable strength, aware that the bracelet of his fingers somehow intensified her pleasure and added an extra dimension to the wildness threatening to overwhelm her.

His big body shuddered beneath her and she saw an untamed challenge in the tawny eyes, yet he still didn't move. Sweat gathered on her temples, between her breasts; the heat in her innermost region began to pulse, to spin into waves, forming and reforming from that central part of her where the only reality was the clenching and relaxing of her muscles on the shaft that penetrated her.

Slowly the relentless inner rhythm built and built until

she could no longer control it, tossing her into a whirlpool of sensation. Yet, although lost in the mindless, private paradise of her response, she heard Clay's long groan and felt the one violent contraction of his body as he reached that place she'd summoned for him.

Exultantly she had time to think, *Yes, this is it, this time the masks are truly off,* before her body twisted, convulsed in intolerable, unbearable pleasure, and she fell forward, caught and held by his hands, lowered against him as his driving heartbeat thundered into her breasts and he dragged breath into parched lungs.

Stunned at the chaos she'd let loose, she lay quiescent, trying desperately to find some stable centre to the whirling disintegration of her world.

Clay's arms were gentle around her, his mouth warm on her forehead. 'Natalia,' he said at last, his voice still raw with the force of passion. 'Natalia...'

This was like heaven, she thought dreamily—like those indolent, flower-filled tropical paradises where sensuality reigned. Alas, like any paradise, a serpent lingered at the heart of it.

When Clay had gone the next morning, she packed the clothes she'd brought with her, leaving everything he'd bought her except the tiny gold lion.

Biting her lip, she looked down at the small charm. 'I'll buy you a witch on a broomstick,' she'd said when he'd dropped it on to her pillow, and he'd laughed.

'And a wardrobe too?'

'Oh, yes, *The Lion, the Witch and the Wardrobe* by C. S. Lewis,' she said. 'I adored the Narnia books.'

'Olivia read them to me when she took me home.' His eyes gleamed. 'I'd like a witch. Or a mask.'

'Why—oh, the masquerade ball.' Sudden moisture had stung her eyes. 'Would you wear a charm if I got you one?'

He'd laughed and promised, 'Next to my heart.'

So Natalia had used her allowance to order both—a tiny,

bare-breasted witch on a broomstick, and a mask; she'd picked them up only the previous day.

Now she slipped all three into her bag.

She wrote a letter. It would have taken even longer than two hours, except that she was afraid Clay might come back and catch her.

Then she picked up the pack containing the clothes she'd brought from Xanadu, walked up to the shops where she used her card to get cash, and took a bus to the depot. There she bought a ticket in a false name to Palmerston North, because no one would ever think of looking for her in that small southern city so far from Auckland.

And from Clay.

CHAPTER ELEVEN

ALTHOUGH it had been raining heavily for the past three days, Natalia hadn't bargained on floods. In fact, the weather seemed so attuned to her mood that at first she'd welcomed the driving rain, but only an hour and a half out of Auckland the bus slowed and stopped in a line of traffic beside the huge Waikato River.

At first she gazed with dull-eyed indifference through the window, but eventually her eyes focused on the bare tops of willows poking up through discoloured water. Her gaze sharpened, for that water flowed with ominous, deceptive smoothness almost at the top of the stopbanks. Working close by, people filled sandbags to reinforce the banks.

Such frail barriers between rich farmland and the muscular brown river!

'I hope we get past.' The elderly man beside her frowned. 'Northbound traffic can't come through, I know, but surely the southbound lane isn't closed too?'

'I didn't realise the river was so close to overtopping the banks,' Natalia said.

He glanced at her a bit oddly, as though wondering what she'd been doing these past few days. 'That rain in the catchment last night was the final straw. It hasn't reached here yet, but it's on the way. The dams are full and Lake Taupo's overfull—they're hoping they don't have to let last night's downpour come through. If they do, these farms are doomed.'

Natalia dragged herself sufficiently out of her misery to ask, 'How much will be flooded?'

'A lot of land,' he said. 'A lot of broken hearts.'

She nodded sombrely. 'I hope they've been able to move their stock.'

'They've known this was coming, so they'll have got them away. I suppose that's some sort of comfort, but I wouldn't want to be in their boots. Still, they've got guts.' He leaned forward to peer past her. 'They're not just sitting back waiting for it to happen. And if it works they'll save a lot of good farmers from losing a lot of money.'

Natalia watched the pattern of movements; one person to hold out the sack, another to shovel in the sand, and then the rhythm of wet, tired arms and bodies moving in a wave as the sandbags were passed along a human chain to the top of the stopbanks, where they were dumped into place.

That was what she needed, she thought. Hard work.

'Can I get past you?' she asked the old man.

He rose stiffly from the seat and stood back to let her out.

She pulled down her pack and went up to the front of the bus. 'I'd like to get off here, please,' she said.

'All right,' the driver said casually, although he made a notation on his manifest before he let her down.

Hours later Natalia was passing sandbags up the stopbank, cursing as the rain drove mercilessly down and hopelessness began to draw the faces of the people around her. News crews came and went, both radio and television, but they didn't go near Natalia so she ignored them, sublimating in exhausting labour the pain that lodged in her throat and squeezed her heart.

And still the rain came and still the river rose, until it was only a foot below the top of the stopbank.

Late in the afternoon the woman beside Natalia told her, 'They're going to let out the dams.'

Natalia shook sand down into the bag and handed it to her. 'What?'

'The hydro-electric dams are too full. They're trying to let the excess out slowly so they don't put too much pressure on the stopbanks.'

She didn't say any more, but she didn't need to. If the

dams were released, the odds were that all this work would be wasted.

'I suppose it was worth a try,' Natalia said dully, stretching her aching arms. A month was all it had taken for her to get out of condition. A month of intense, distilled joy that she was going to live off for the rest of her life. Her eyes burned as she shovelled sand into yet another bag.

The woman shrugged, her short grey hair dank and draggled under her rainproof hat. 'That's all anyone can do,' she said calmly. 'Trying beats not trying any day.'

For some reason her words echoed in Natalia's brain as an early dusk fell heavily about them. Had she given up too easily?

'You're looking pretty tired,' one man said to her at last, shining a torch into her face. 'Where are you staying?'

'I don't know.'

He nodded, not startled. She wasn't the only person who'd felt compelled to stop and help. 'The marae is open all night,' he said. 'Grab a bed there.'

The marae—the meeting place of the local Maori people, a complex of buildings set up with sleeping and dining halls around a ceremonial open place—was on the top of a low rise. Its committee had opened it for the workers; the dining hall had been where she'd forced herself to swallow some food several hours ago.

She'd go later. Ignoring the protest of abused muscles, Natalia fell back into the rhythm of filling and handing on, filling and handing on...

When a vehicle drew up behind her and she heard her name, she automatically swung around. Clay, tall and dark and grim, those lion's eyes flat and deadly, got down from a four-wheel drive.

'What the *hell* are you doing here?' he demanded furiously.

'Working,' Natalia said huskily, her heart leaping to meet him. 'How did you know I was here?'

'Television. I recognised you in a long shot.' Clay's

hooded eyes devoured her face as he reined in his anger. 'You're exhausted.'

'Tired,' she admitted.

'All right, get in.'

The weariness she'd been fighting suddenly overwhelmed her. She staggered, and Clay caught her, his arms tight and hard around her.

'That's it,' he said wrathfully. 'You're out of here.'

She let him bundle her into the vehicle out of the rain and slam the door on her. Someone pointed out her pack, and he threw that in the back. Needles of rain slanted relentlessly down as he strode around the front of the vehicle and got in.

Without speaking, he put the vehicle in gear and set off down the road, past the marae—

'Hey,' she exclaimed hoarsely, adrenaline surging through her, 'that's where I'm going to sleep.'

'If the stopbanks go the marae might too. I want you well away if that happens.'

Natalia looked at a profile carved in stone, every angle and plane imperviously carved. He wasn't going to give an inch. 'I'm not going back to Auckland,' she said stubbornly.

'I'm not either—the less time we spend on the road in this weather the better. I've booked us in into a hotel on the Thames road.' His voice was cool, remote and utterly inflexible.

Natalia chewed her lip. The previous night she'd been making love to him as a farewell gift; now she felt as foolish as an angry child brought back home after running away. 'I meant what I said in my letter,' she said after a moment.

'"*Dear Clay, I'm sorry but I don't want to stay with you any longer. Thank you for everything you've done for me—I really appreciate your kindness. Yours sincerely, Natalia,*"' he quoted cruelly. 'It read like a kid's bread-and-butter letter.'

'What did you expect—half a book?' she flashed.

Oncoming car lights caught his face in a swift murderous

grin. 'That sounds more like the Natalia I know. Tell me why you took off after that bravura performance last night.'

She summoned her sweetest tone. 'Sometimes it must occur to men that sex isn't the only important thing in a relationship. I know it doesn't happen often, but surely it does occasionally.'

To her profound fury he laughed. She jerked up against the seat belt, bitterly aware that she'd come alive again, that his presence would probably call her from her grave. He was so vital, burning with a fierce contained energy that struck sparks from her. She'd resigned herself to never feeling like this again, and it was tearing at her because she was going to have to say goodbye to him once more.

'Oh, it occurs to us now and then,' he drawled, 'but you must admit that you weren't thinking of anything else last night, and neither was I. By the time you'd reached my chest with those infuriating little caresses, it was all I could do not to throw you down flat and sink myself into you for as long as I could last. The only thing that kept me sane was the fact that I knew you felt the same.'

She didn't answer, and he asked with a sudden savage fury, 'Why the hell did you take off today?'

A voice echoed in Natalia's mind, a voice she'd heard often that day, and always with a kind of resigned strength. 'Trying beats not trying,' the woman had said once, and those words had sunk into Natalia's brain.

If I don't try now, she thought, I'll never know.

She said, 'I—want more than you can give me.'

'More what?'

She didn't blame him for his exasperation. 'I'm making a hash of this.'

'And you must be bloody near exhausted,' he said curtly. 'Leave it for now—we're almost there. We'll wait until tomorrow and then we'll talk. But no more running away, all right?'

'All right,' she said.

There was a moment's silence before he asked, 'Promise?'

'Yes,' she said, her heart twisting. 'I promise.'

The hotel turned out to be a far cry from the double-storeyed Victorian building she'd expected; he'd booked them into a modern resort set amongst trees and vineyards in a valley that faced the west. Had Natalia been less tired she might have been self-conscious at her condition; even through her fatigue she was glad that the desk clerk and porter were too well-trained to show any surprise at the layer of mud and sand that covered her.

Once they'd been shown to their room Clay ordered, 'Into the shower.'

She obeyed, walking fully-clothed into the stall, sighing with intense relief as the warm water cascaded over her aching body. After several minutes Clay got in with her, matter-of-factly removing her clothes.

'Warm enough?' he asked.

'Yes.' And the muscles that had stiffened in the car ride were now deliciously loose again.

'OK, out you get.' He rubbed her down briskly with a towel, then picked her up and carried her into the bedroom. He'd spread a white bath sheet on the bed. Lowering her on to it, he said, 'They do a nice line in toiletries here. I'll work some of the knots out of your shoulders.'

Tiredness and simple gratitude at being cared for kept her silent and limp as he smoothed warm oil that smelt of lavender into her skin, and then with strong hands massaged her shoulders and back and hips, the long muscles of her thighs, and even her upper arms.

When her muscles had dissolved into jelly and she'd been reduced to a collection of responses, he switched off the light, tucked her into bed, and got in beside her, saying, 'Sleep now.'

It was still dark when she woke, and the radio was on. Locked in Clay's arms, she listened as the announcer continued, '...the stopbanks were overtopped. Flooding is widespread, and it's expected that the farms will be underwater for anything up to two weeks. However, forecasters believe that the worst of the weather is over, and the high now on its way across the Tasman Sea should ensure several days of fine weather.'

Clay moved and the radio clicked off. Natalia couldn't stop the slow build of tears, the choking gasp against his warmth.

'I'm sorry,' he said roughly, kissing the top of her head. 'I know how hard you worked for those people. When you do something you fling your heart and soul into it.'

'I'm sorry for them,' she said, wiping her eyes with her hand, 'but not sorry I tried. A woman there said that trying beats not trying.' She paused, aware of the stirring of his body, the physical signs of need he never tried to hide. Even if he didn't love her, surely he felt something more for her than uncomplicated lust?

'You've always been a trier.' His voice rumbled against the persistent chattering of the rain on the roof. 'I wanted you the first time I saw you, but I think it was your obstinate, pig-headed determination that got to me. I couldn't see how anyone as delicate and sexy as you could be so determined and stubborn. I knew I should stay away from you, but I couldn't.'

'Why should you have stayed away—oh, of course. Dean,' she said, stiffening.

Firmly tucking her back against him, he said, 'I saw you first when I looked out of the land agent's office in April, about two months before we met at the masquerade ball, and you were outside talking to Phil. You laughed. And the land agent said that you were a very generous girl, and that you'd had an affair with Dean. He also insinuated that you were looking for someone to get you out of the hole you were in.'

'The slimy old toad!' she exclaimed.

'I shut him up,' he said indifferently, 'but I bought Pukekahu partly because of your laugh.'

'Not to pay Dean back?'

She felt his crooked smile. 'Oh, that too. I was still hung up on taking everything away from him that I could.'

Fear crawled across her tentative hope on slimy feet. No, she thought; I will not let Dean's insinuations smirch what Clay and I have. 'And now?'

'Now it doesn't seem important at all.' He seemed to be thinking as he went, as though he was facing up to this for the first time. 'I wanted Pukekahu because Olivia loved it. She used to tell me all about it, about how happy she'd been there. I couldn't believe that she'd left it to Dean when she knew—she had to know—he wouldn't value it. He hated her almost as much as he hates me.'

During that long, gruelling afternoon, Natalia had thought a lot about his mother's astonishing decision. 'What would have happened if she'd left Pukekahu to you?'

After a moment he said, 'I'd have worked it, of course.'

'Without capital?'

He paused, then said, 'I'd have made a success of it eventually.'

'But even before Dean did his best to run it into the ground it was in a mess, wasn't it? Olivia's father—old Mr Freeman—was in real financial trouble long before he died.'

'I'd have brought it back into full production.' He sounded impatient. 'Olivia must have known I'd do that for her, if for no other reason.'

Natalia nodded. 'Of course she knew you'd have been loyal enough to stick it out to the end, and you'd eventually have made a go of it.' It was impossible to imagine Clay failing, once he'd set his formidable will to a project. 'But it had been neglected for over twenty years, and you'd have been trapped in exactly the same situation I was at Xanadu. Debts, and no money. Olivia was a farmer's daughter, a farmer's wife—she understood what lack of capital does to a farmer. And if she'd left both Pukekahu and the money to you, what would have happened?'

Clay didn't answer for so long she wondered whether he'd fallen asleep. Eventually he said in a low, harsh voice, 'My stepfather would have contested the will. He told me it was only the fact that the money she'd left to me came from a family trust—so he couldn't get his hands on it in any case—that stopped him from doing that. And he thought he had the better of it, anyway—he knew what Pukekahu meant to me.'

'Exactly,' Natalia said, convinced now that she was right. Speaking urgently, she went on, 'By leaving the station to Dean, she made sure you kept the money and didn't waste it on lawyer's fees fighting to keep Pukekahu. Clay, she *knew* you, and she loved you. She *knew* you'd use the legacy of money to make a life for yourself. That's why she left Pukekahu to Dean—so that you had the chance to follow your own dreams, not be tied to hers.' She hesitated, then said into the cool darkness, 'That's an awe-inspiring gift. I wish I'd known her.'

Another long silence, until he said in a rough, shaken voice, 'You could be right. She told me just before she died that she'd left things so that I'd never have to go cap in hand to anyone.'

'She gave you the chance to be whatever you wanted to be, and the freedom to do whatever you wanted,' Natalia said.

'Unlike your father.' His tone was even, without inflection.

She said quietly, 'Unlike my father. He didn't intend to die, of course—'

'But he didn't give you any chance to follow your own star.'

'No,' she said in a muffled voice.

Clay's arms contracted around her. Into her hair he said with difficulty, 'I think you're right about Olivia. And she might have meant to explain it before she died, but when it came it was sudden, and I was at boarding school. I should have trusted her. What I saw as her treachery ate into me, made me doubt her love—but she'd have known what my stepfather was likely to do. She had no illusions about him, or Dean.' He kissed her. 'Thank you.'

Her body stirred; she kissed him back and smiled sadly into the darkness as she felt him respond. Did she love him enough to stay with him?

Would he ever trust a woman? He'd been let down so often—by his birth mother, by the mother of his heart—*could* he learn to trust enough to love?

His chest lifted in noiseless laughter. 'If I'd come to Pukekahu then, I'd have known you fourteen years ago.'

'I wasn't there when I was nine,' she returned drily. 'And you wouldn't have been interested anyway.'

'I'll bet I'd have noticed when you grew up. I'd have been your first lover.'

'That's an arrogant statement. Does it worry you that you weren't?'

He paused before saying quietly, 'I wish I could say no, of course it doesn't. It's never bothered me with other women, but with you all sorts of primitive feelings surface.' He slid a hand across her breasts, cupping them.

'Very primitive,' she managed to say as anticipation geared up a notch.

'I'd like to have been your first and only lover, but I'm not crazily jealous of the boy you loved when you were eighteen.' His voice was slow and reflective, as slow as the gentle movement of his thumbs across the heated peaks of her breasts.

Natalia's breath caught in her throat. Lazy fire coiled away from beneath his touch, flowed through nerve-cells, along the secret pathways of her body, stripping away everything but her need for him, for the powerful mastery of his body, for the intense pleasure only he could give her.

Yet, exquisite though this was, she needed more from him than the sex.

His voice deepened, became a little raw, a little rough. 'Every time I look at you I have to stop myself from dragging you off to bed. Even when you were talking to Phil outside the land agent's office in Bowden! It didn't help when I discovered that as well as fuelling my hottest dreams you had a sharp tongue and an even sharper brain.' He paused, then added, 'I wanted you at the masquerade ball, but when I saw how hard you worked to pay a debt that wasn't even morally yours because you didn't want an elderly couple to suffer—that's when I fell in love with you.'

Her breath hurt in her lungs; she whispered, 'I don't believe you.'

'I'm not surprised. It took me quite some time to accept that that's what it is—love. At first I thought I was obsessed with a woman who slept with anyone she thought might help her out financially, or perhaps one who just enjoyed sex for sex's sake.'

His words battered her like a blunt instrument. 'Then why did you offer to pay my debts?' she asked gruffly. 'Were you testing me?'

He moved slightly in the warmth, his voice reflective. 'I hated to see you working so hard. I wanted to snatch you up and take you away, shower you with everything you needed to make you happy, wrap you in silk and jewels and spoil you to death. By the time we went out to dinner at The Indies I didn't care whether you loved me or simply saw me as a good bet. I'd have taken anything you offered. But you didn't offer, although I knew damned well that you wanted me. Instead, you delivered a passionate little speech on how you wanted your freedom.'

'I remember.' She kissed his shoulder, trying to find the right way to tell him that it didn't matter now, that the best sort of freedom would be to live with him and love him.

Clay's body tensed, but he continued, 'The worst of it was, I could understand perfectly, but by that time I was beginning to realise that I wanted to tie you down and never let you go.' Beneath the note of irony in his words there was a raw hunger that sent a frisson scudding down Natalia's spine. 'So when the thieves moved in, and Phil had his brainstorm and slashed off the capsicum plants, I was glad, because it meant I could take you away from it all.'

'I don't think I've ever been so torn and desperate,' she said. About a fortnight after they'd left for Auckland the police had rung to say they'd caught the thieves who'd stolen the fencing materials and the computer—a well-organised ring who preyed on farmers.

Clay kissed her again, his hands still lightly brushing over her nipples. 'I knew that, and I used it quite ruthlessly. I was determined to have you. I hoped that living with me would show you that you were a little bit in love with me. And until this morning I thought I was succeeding.'

'You succeeded only too well,' she told him dreamily.

'Yet you took off this morning as though it meant nothing! When I got home—it seems a year ago!—I couldn't believe you'd gone. Why, Natalia? Did you believe Dean when he said I only wanted you because he did too?'

'As much as you did,' she said. 'Of course I didn't. I left you because I'm hopelessly, irrevocably, wildly in love with you, and I thought you only wanted the better class of mistress I taunted you with when we first met. I felt as though we'd met with masks on, and we'd never really taken them off, and that if I couldn't have everything it was safer to have nothing. In other words, I ran away like a coward.'

'Would you have ever come back to me?'

She hesitated, then, without any thought of qualification, gave him the surrender he wanted so much. 'Yes. I love you. Leaving you tore my heart out.'

He slid his questing hand down to her hip, stroked the satin skin on the inside of her thigh. After a moment he said thickly, 'I wouldn't have stopped looking until I'd found you. I need you so much. Nothing is worthwhile if you're not with me, if I can't come home to that wicked smile and those tantalising green eyes, if I don't know that at the end of the day we'll sit together and talk. Making love to you is undeserved heaven, but I value all the other things about you as much—your quick intelligence, your energy, your obstinate determination to do what you think is right, your rock-solid integrity. Natalia, sweet witch, marry me soon.'

'Of course I'll marry you,' she said softly, her body lax and contented against his. She reached up and kissed the determined chin. 'I think I fell in love with you when you carried me up the steps and told me I was like jasmine, beautiful and a survivor.'

'Speaking of flowers, how bad is your allergy to wasps?'

'I have to take the pills with me wherever I go, but I'm usually very careful—except when my brain is being scrambled by the man next door.' She kissed him again, shivering when his arms tightened around her. 'Thank heavens you saw me on television.'

'Mmm. When I found you'd gone I went berserk. I called the police and a detective agency, and demanded that they start looking for you straight away.' He nuzzled her cheek, found the corner of her mouth and kissed it. 'Then I saw you on the news and burnt up the road getting there. Fortunately for my sanity I'd already worked out that if I couldn't find you I'd have to fly across to see your friend Liz and plead with her to tell me where you were.'

'She'd probably have spilled the beans,' Natalia said, laughing a little wryly. 'She thinks you're gorgeous.'

'Hmm. She's very protective of you.' But his voice was smooth and amused. It altered, however, when he said, 'What do you want to do after we're married? Go to university? Live in the country? Get your own business?'

'What I *should* do,' she said vengefully, 'is go back to Bowden and set up as a land agent next to that wretched Sam Phillips. If he hadn't been such a nasty old gossip you wouldn't have thought I was a reincarnation of Cleopatra.'

He laughed. 'Oh, I think I would have.' He paused, then said quietly, 'I didn't know it then, but I don't think I had much faith in women until I met you.'

'I'm not surprised.' Natalia hugged him suddenly. 'Your birth mother's cruelty must have affected you, and then she died; it's a kind of betrayal, isn't it, when your parent dies? And then you thought Olivia had betrayed you all over again, leaving Pukekahu to Dean. You don't get over those things quickly, or easily.'

Clay said unevenly, 'I didn't get over them until I met you and discovered that there were women who kept the faith, who lived up to their responsibilities.'

When she kissed his eyes, her mouth found damp lashes. A shaft of emotion, slightly maternal for the child he'd been, wholly adult for the man he was now, transfixed her. She whispered, 'I love you so much.'

'And I love you, with all that I am, all that I'll ever be.'

All barriers down, they lay locked in the silent communion of a close embrace, until Clay said, 'Listen.'

She listened, and realised that the rain had eased, and a small wind was making its way around the corners of the building. 'The wind's changed,' she said, a sudden blaze of joy bursting through her.

'Mmm.' He sounded lazy and replete. 'Do you want to take that botany degree you planned at school?'

She shook her head. 'I love drawing the plants, not studying them.'

'Now that,' he said thoughtfully, 'you could do if you travelled with me—I move around quite a lot. You could be as independent as you liked, provided you came back to me each night.'

It sounded like heaven. 'I'd like that.'

'Good. There's no hurry, but I think your talent for drawing will show you the right path for you. Where do you want to live?'

She hesitated, then asked, 'How about Pukekahu?'

'We could,' he said. And, with the astuteness that sometimes made her just a little afraid of him, he added, 'By the way, Phil's gone. He's got a job on a sheep station in the South Island high country.'

'Did you organise it?'

'In a way.'

'I hope he's all right,' she said.

'He'll be fine. He just needs time to get over you.' Clay kissed her properly, then to her outrage settled her back in his arms. 'Get some more sleep.'

'Why?' She stretched languorously, rubbing herself lightly against him. 'I don't think I need sleep.'

'You must be exhausted. The muscles on your back were really knotted.'

She sighed elaborately. 'I believe the best way to work stiffness out of muscles is to use them again.'

'How could I have forgotten?' he said with silky distinctness, and bent his head to whisper dark words of passion in her ear.

Natalia abandoned herself to the mindless tide of desire. Outside the rain had begun again, but now it fell quietly, gently, and in the darkened bedroom they made love with all the promise and joy of a future filled with summer.

EPILOGUE

EVERY year in spring, when the gardens around the homestead were hung with roses and starred with daylilies and irises and the first gardenias, the Beauchamps held a special garden party on the wide lawns of Pukekahu for close friends. It was always a joyous occasion, and this time especially so; Liz was back from England.

But then, Clay thought, waking soon after dawn, it was always a joyous occasion to wake next to his wife.

He turned his head, smiling at the tumble of black curls on Natalia's pillow. Eyes still closed, she responded to his movement, snuggling into his waiting arms.

She did it every morning, as though even in her deepest sleep she was aware of him. He listened to the steady beat of her heart under his hand, felt the tiny flexions of her muscles as she stumbled into wakefulness.

After a while she muttered, 'Darling,' into his chest.

'Good morning,' he said, smoothing back one defiant curl to kiss her ear. 'Do you realise it's exactly two years, three months and one week since I managed to persuade you to give up your freedom for me?'

He loved it when she laughed. A secret, smoky little sound, it went right to the roots of his being, warming some cold part of him that never quite believed his luck.

'A wonderful two years, three months and one week,' she murmured, stretching seductively against him. 'I think we can say that this is one physical attraction that's lasted, don't you?'

Lasted? 'It feels that way,' he said gravely, cupping the smooth, warm, soft curve of her breast. 'Happy, Ms Artist?'

Soon after they'd married, Clay had introduced his wife

to close friends, one of whom worked for a publisher. Entranced by the sketches Natalia had done, he'd mentioned them to his boss. Serendipitously, they'd been exactly what was wanted for a picture book, so she and the author, the mother of three children, had co-operated for a frustrating, exhilarating, enjoyable few months. The book had come out just in time for the Christmas market.

Her mouth tilted in the enchanting, seductively mischievous smile she reserved only for him. 'More than happy, darling,' she said, her voice a little huskier than usual.

'So am I. You look,' Clay said, 'infinitely more beautiful than when we first made love in this room.' He kissed a certain spot on her shoulder that drove her crazy, but didn't follow through. Instead, he lifted his head to look around. 'Mind you,' he said, 'the room looks infinitely more beautiful than it did then too.'

'Because you were determined to have your ivory and green room,' Natalia said through a yawn. 'I'm so glad we decided not to demolish the homestead. Whenever I come into this room I look around and remember the first time I slept here. A new house just wouldn't bring back the same memories.'

It had cost far more to rebuild and renovate the homestead than it would have to build a modern house of the same size. 'My one act of sentiment,' Clay said lightly.

'What about the jasmine?'

The jasmine still flourished, much to the disapproval of the married couple who kept the gardens in manicured condition. 'It keeps the house together,' he said. 'Besides, I remember carrying you up the steps the night we first made love, with the jasmine scenting the air.'

Yawning, Natalia kissed his shoulder, then bit it in gentle contemplation. 'Two acts of sentiment,' she murmured against his skin.

Her touch, the warmth of her slender body in his arms, the faint female perfume that rose from her skin and hair, the silken slide of her skin against his—all worked their inevitable magic on him. Tamping down the fumes of desire that began to clog his brain, he laughed under his breath and twisted to reach something on his side table. 'And here's another,' he said, dropping a small gold charm on her breast: a tiny open book.

'Darling, thank you,' Natalia said in a voice rich with love. She narrowed her eyes at him. 'Though why I should wear them when you won't wear the little witch and the mask I bought you, I don't know.'

He grinned. 'I carry the witch in my chest pocket; that's next to my heart. And I prefer to see you wearing the others.'

After a short, but very satisfactory interval, Natalia sat up and hooked her arms around her bare knees, smiling at the sun that poured in through the French windows. With a swift sideways glance she said, 'You know, this book of mine has given me ideas. Now that it's sold to England and America, I thought I'd like to do a picture book for babies. But I need a model. Shall we try for one?'

Clay felt the impact of her words right through to his soul. 'Are you sure?' he asked, controlling his response.

She turned to him, the gleam of provocation in her green eyes fading. Very seriously she said, 'Only if you want them.'

He had to pause, to choose his words carefully. 'I want them,' he said, 'but children tie chains around your heart, around your life. They're just as efficient a trap as a horticultural unit with a huge mortgage.' He'd never suggested them because his lovely, talented, magnificent Natalia needed as much freedom as he could give her.

'I don't feel trapped in our marriage,' she said, not looking at him. Her lashes were dark fans against her ivory skin, her full, soft mouth a little compressed.

Clay repressed a surge of aching love, of desire, to listen as she went on, 'When we first met the physical attraction was so strong that it swamped everything else; it terrified me, because how could I know whether it would last, whether it had any sort of solid foundation? But as well as setting my body on fire you were kind and thoughtful and intelligent and interesting and honourable, and I fell in love. Only deep inside I still wondered. I thought it might be a kind of obsession, that one day I might wake up and it would be gone.'

'I guessed,' he said, suddenly cold, fighting a stark, hungry need to take her in his arms and kiss her, turn her mindless with lust, secure her to him in the one way that never failed.

A smile wavered on her lips; she turned to him, her exotic eyes sparkling with tears. 'Clay, during these past two years, three months and one week I've realised two things—that the desire is part of love, not something separate and untrustworthy, and that the freedom I wanted so much was the freedom to be with you, to make a life together. And I'd like children to be part of that life.'

It was the surrender he'd waited for, the last barrier shattered.

Yet surrender was the wrong word. Unable to find words, Clay leaned over and pulled her into his arms. As always, she came willingly, her body pliant, her response immediate and unfettered.

He said harshly, 'We'll give them the best we can, my heart. Everything good your parents did, everything good Olivia did for me—we'll make mistakes, but our children will always know we love them.'

They'd come full circle, back to Pukekahu, back to love and trust and the promise of all that they'd missed—a family, a home, a place in each other's heart that was inviolable. As she kissed the rough silk of his jaw, Natalia knew that they had found their refuge, their reason for loving, the dream both had sought so long without knowing it.

And before she surrendered to passion's honeyed lure, she thanked both her father and Olivia for setting into motion the events that had led to this.

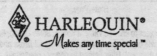